WHIRLWIND

(When Lust turns to Love)

by

Jerry Russell

Published April 2015 by
South Oxford Press
Oxford, NY 13830

ISBN-13: 978-0692424308
ISBN-10: 069242430X

2015
South Oxford Press
2139 County Road 3
Oxford, NY 13830
email: southoxfordpress@live.com.

PREFACE

This is a semi-fictional 'Romantica' novel.

'Romantica' is a melding of romantic and erotic, with the premise that the novel will have a romantic ending.

This novel is semi-fictional, because it is a blending of a real-life situation, observed by the author, and the fantasies of the author's imagination. The descriptions of the two main characters intimate relations are clearly descriptive and erotic.

It is a story of two people meeting in a work environment, and how events in their personal lives led to a short lustful period. Subsequent events changed their lustful arrangement into a partnership of love. The story takes the reader through their adventure and describes how it led to a romantic ending.

* * * WEEK ONE * * *

LUST

CHAPTER - 1

It was a slow day in the Space Research Lab. Most of the engineers and techs had gone out to lunch. I had just finished a sandwich that I had brought from home and decided to wander up to the mail boxes.

Calling them mail boxes was being generous. It was really an assembly of pigeonholes bolted to the wall.

I was pretty new to the lab, and I hadn't met everyone yet, so it was a pleasant surprise to see a gorgeous young blonde standing at the mail station.

"No mail again." she said, to no one in particular. "No one ever sends me any mail. I guess no one likes me."

"Hi, I'm Jerry Fox" I said. "I'm new here." Which of course, she probably already knew. What she didn't know was that I had this feeling of a sudden 'awakening' in the front of my pants. I just hoped that it wasn't too obvious.

"I'm Becky" she said. "Rebecca Blake, nice to meet you. What project are you working on?"

"I'm starting work on the new satellite imaging program." I said. "I was working over in the Electronics Lab, on the main campus, but they were looking for engineers for this project and it sounded interesting, so here I am."

"What do you do here?" I asked.

"I'm a senior computer programmer and I manage the SSDI main frame computer for the lab." she said.

"Oh, great, maybe you could help me learn FORTRAN programming. A part of my work is going to be a computer analysis of the data that comes back from the satellite. So the earlier I start to learn the language, the quicker I can show some results from the project."

"I'd be happy to help you" said Becky. "When would you like to start?"

"The sooner, the better. I have some free time this afternoon, if you could spare an hour or two."

"Perfect." said Becky, "How about 3 O'clock? We can work for a couple of hours."

"OK, I'll come down to your office at 3. See you then."

CHAPTER 2

A few minutes before 3, I picked up a pad of paper and a few pencils and started down the outside hallway towards Becky's office. I had taken the time to do some reconnaissance and knew exactly where her office was located and the easiest way to get there.

Knock, knock. I tapped on her door.

"Come in, Jerry." she said.

"Have a seat at the table; we can work together more easily there."

As she sat down next to me, her leg brushed up against mine, and it was like a lightning bolt had hit me. Was that accidental, I wondered, but then she instantly got to the business of programming, with no mention of the 'accidental' touching.

"I believe you said you wanted to learn FORTRAN," said Becky, "which would be FORTRAN IV. I think that is the best for your work. It is the easiest to work with. I do my work in COBOL, but that is a machine language and much more difficult to learn. FORTRAN makes it easier for you to write data analysis programs."

"In either case, once you have written the lines of your program, you have to go to the punch-card machine and make cards for the computer to read your program. Once you feed those into the computer and you know that the program runs properly, you can generate a magnetic tape on a reel to use for continuing work."

"OK." I said, "How do we start?"

And what a start. Three hours later we had gotten through the fundamentals of FORTRAN and I had written my first, very simple, test program. Tomorrow I would make the punch-cards and try running it on the computer. But for now my mind was too full of computer language to work anymore.

"Whew!" I said. "I knew this was going to be time consuming, but we sure got through three hours in a flash. I really appreciate this help and I'm looking forward to learning more and becoming better."

"Well," said Becky, "this was just the basics so far. There are a lot of tricks and tools that will make your task easier once you learn them."

"I didn't realize how late it was getting." I replied. "I'm getting hungry, and my wife is out of town visiting her parents, so I'm going to eat out. Could I talk you into joining me and maybe we could cover some more programming? I would be happy to treat, since you have been so helpful."

"Well, that is coincidental." said Becky, "My husband, Jack, happens to be away at a mathematics conference this week. He's an assistant professor here at the University. And I'm not too interested in cooking just for myself. I would be glad to join you for dinner."

"Great!" I said, as the front of my pants tightened up again. "There is this little Italian restaurant just outside of town that I really like. Would that be alright?"

"Absolutely," she said, "I love Italian food, and maybe they even serve liquor, because I could use a drink to help me relax a little. I get so hyped up working on new projects."

"I'll give them a call and make sure we can get a quiet table. Do you want me to pick you up at your house, or leave your car here and pick it up later? The restaurant, which I have in mind, is over on this side of town."

"Let's leave my car here. Since I live on the other side of town, I'll pick it up after we finish.

As I was heading for the door, to go to my office, Becky touched my arm and said "I'm going to go into the ladies room and freshen up a bit while you call the restaurant."

I know it probably was just an innocent touch, but it felt like a lightning bolt, and the front of my pants started to expand as I walked down the hall to my office. 'Control yourself, I said, she is married and probably happily so. Don't get any wild expectations.'

CHAPTER 3

"I should have known we were going to Luigi's." said Becky, "I haven't been here in a very long time, but I know the food is great and the atmosphere is nice and subdued."

"*Gooda evening, folks.*" Luigi, greeted us as we entered and showed us to a nice quiet table in the back. It was a week night so business was a little slow.

The waitress came right over and Becky ordered a Chivas Regal on the rocks, which is my favorite drink, so I felt a little self-conscious when I ordered the same.

We made small talk, learning a little about each other, as we sipped our drinks. We had both ordered the chicken Marsala and laughed together about our similar tastes.

As I was mentioning my Marine Corps service and showed her my Marine Corps ring, she took my fingers in her hand so she could examine the ring more carefully. 'Damn, another bolt of lightning. Why are my pants getting so tight?'

"I knew there was something special about you when I first saw you." said Becky,

"Now I know what it is. You're a big bad Marine."

Now my pants definitely were becoming a bit snug. Was I just imagining that something was happening between us?

After dinner we had another drink while sitting in the lounge in front of the fireplace and sitting a little closer.

As I turned to Becky, I said "I really appreciate your taking all this time with me today. I really didn't expect so much help so soon, especially from a drop-dead gorgeous woman."

As I finished my little speech, Becky turned towards me and met my lips with hers. It seemed that she held the kiss forever, and as a further complication her right hand found my leg and worked its way up to my crotch, which by now was in a state of full arousal.

As we came up for air, she said: "I should have mentioned that Chivas Regal makes me really 'hot' and your manliness has just put me over the top. Would you like to find a more private place to continue?"

And I readily agreed.

I got up, though self-conscious about the bulge in the front of my pants, found a phone and made a call to a nearby Red Roof Inn, where I booked a room for the night.

CHAPTER 4

The room wasn't real stylish, but it had everything we needed, a bed, and a shower.

As soon as I had locked the door, I pulled Becky into my arms and kissed her long and hard, and it was returned in full by her.

As we came up for air, I said: "I really would like to take a shower. Would you care to wash my back?"

"I could use a shower, too," said Becky, "and I'll wash yours if you'll wash mine." 'Hmm! was she referring to our backs, or ...?'

Not wasting any time we got out of our clothes, stepped into the shower and proceeded to lather up. I could easily see that her clothed beauty was far exceeded by her raw beauty and I got harder with the promise of what was to come.

I went first, washing her back, all the way down, kissing her butt as I washed her legs and feet, then her front, starting with her breasts, which were a little on the small size, but upright and taught, with hard nipples. I was tempted to spend more time on them, but soon worked my way down between her legs to what I found was a 'hot-spot' with very fine soft blond hair (a natural blonde) and a steaming hot twot.

Dropping to my knees, I proceeded to 'clean it' with my tongue, as she cried out in pleasure and gripped my head. But too soon she pulled me up, saying that it was her turn.

She proceeded to wash my back, then my front, starting at my chest and quickly working her way down to my already erect and straining manhood. After giving it a good scrubbing and rinsing, she dropped to her knees and took me in her mouth, almost all of me, but I was so aroused she would have had to have been a sword swallower to take it all in.

As she worked on me, I had to lean against the wall and grip her head to stay upright. My legs were getting weak and I didn't know how long I could stay standing.

Becky worked on me for only a few minutes and I could feel myself coming to a peak. It didn't take long and I had to let her have it. It was just what she wanted. She sucked me dry, until my dong went limp or halfway there, anyway.

Climbing over the edge of the tub wasn't easy after that, for either of us, but as we dried each other off, we both started to get excited again. Rubbing that towel over her breasts was really a turn on for me. They weren't large, but they were so nicely proportioned and just right for sucking, which I did standing there alongside the tub. I love to suck tits. Not quite as much as I like sucking pussy, but still good.

While I was working on her tits, she was drying off my pride and joy, which, surprisingly, was also responding. I guess the many days of abstinence had to be made up. And Becky's touch seemed to provide some magical elixir.

Helping each other into the bedroom wasn't the easiest task, because neither one of us wanted to let go, but somehow we made it to the bed and pulled back the covers to get to the clean sheets.

As we got into the bed, I made the first move, going back to work on her tits, like a baby needing milk. And her nipples were so upright and tight, I couldn't resist moving back and forth between them.

Finally I started working my way down her stomach, kissing as I went, until I got to the treasure. As I began to lick and kiss around, it was obvious that she was more than ready. Her pussy was swollen and hot, and juice was already running down her legs. I put my tongue to good use licking up some of that juice, working my way to my real goal, her swollen pussy lips, which I proceeded to take in my mouth and suck and lick at the same time. Then I began to explore her inner regions with my tongue, searching for her clit, nibbling at the same time, waiting to see what reaction I might get.

By this time, Becky was almost out of control, writhing around on the bed, finally locking her legs around my head and pulling me in as tight as she could. After only a few minutes there was a giant shudder and she went stiff, stretching out as far as she could. Then slowly a relaxing of her and her legs, and I could finally breathe again. I guess I had gotten the combination to her 'treasure chest' just right.

With all this going on, I had even forgotten my own predicament with my 'prong' sticking into the sheets under me. I'm surprised that I hadn't blown all by myself.

But, thank goodness, Becky hadn't forgotten me. As I worked my way back up to her tits, and then a long kiss, Becky started working her way down my body until she got to my problem. Licking my dick up and down didn't help my predicament, but it sure felt good. After giving it a good 'cleaning', she went back to work to see how much she could swallow, which really raised my interest as well as the stature of my prick.

But after making sure that I was properly 'raised' she proceeded to get up on her knees and slowly lower herself on me, massaging my balls as she did this. Then leaning over she whispered: "Don't get concerned about 'protection', I'm on the pill. Just lay back and enjoy it."

Then she proceeded to work slowly up and down, up and down, rotating a little each time, and squeezing her pussy together around my prick. OH! What a sensation! It had been a long time since I had been with anyone who could fuck like that. Having been 'drained' only a half hour earlier, I wasn't about to blow my load too quickly now, so I

21

started working with her, lifting her with my hips, rubbing in and out, and trying to extend myself a little further into her each time.

After some time (who the hell can tell how much time has passed in a situation like this) we both started to get a little more urgency until we both said, *"NOW! NOW!"*, and really started pumping until we both climaxed together, lasting for what seemed like a minute.

Finally Becky fell off me onto the bed, stretching out for a few seconds, then turned on her side towards me, and cuddled up with her lips on my neck, murmuring sighs of happiness.

"That was so great." she sighed. "I haven't been sucked and fucked so well in so long, I can't remember the last time. Do we have to stop?"

"I don't have any place to go. No one is home waiting for me and won't be for a week." I said. "We probably just need to get back to the office early so your car being there without you doesn't start gossip. They have a free breakfast here, so I can go down and get us coffee and something to eat when they open."

"That will work for me." she said. "I have a change of clothes at work, in case I need to travel suddenly, so I can change clothes when we get in."

I got up, made sure the door was locked, turned out the lights, got back into bed and pulled the sheet up over us.

Turning towards Becky, I couldn't keep my hands off her, even though I knew I wouldn't be able to 'perform' for a while, after two episodes like we had just had.

She in turn tried to bring me back 'from the dead', without much success. Finally, we just lay there in each other's arms and went to sleep.

CHAPTER 5. - Tuesday

When I woke up, I checked my watch and saw that it was 5 am. And by some miracle, I had 'come back to life' with 'morning wood'. Not wanting to waste the 'event', I turned towards Becky, who was still sound asleep, and gently began rubbing her nipples, then slowly ran my fingers down her belly, ending up in the soft, fine hair around her pussy. Slowly inserting a finger, then two, into her and gently massaging, I could feel her coming awake and responding.

As Becky realized what was happening she began responding with soft moans, then she slid one hand over onto my leg and worked it up to my groin and said: "*OH MY! what a nice surprise*," when she found what was waiting for her. All of a sudden she was wide awake and began massaging me lightly. This in turn got me more active with her and for a few minutes we practiced a bit of mutual masturbation.

Then passion took control again and I rolled over on top of her, putting my prick at the entrance to her honey pot. Without any words she just took control and guided me into her well lubricated pussy, and away we went. I couldn't control myself, as ready as I was, and she was like a bucking bronco. I was giving her as much as I had and she wanted more, so I kept exploring with my prick trying to find the release button in her. All of a sudden she said: "*THERE! THERE! KEEP IT THERE!*" so I did, and in moments I felt her building up to an explosion, so I concentrated on keeping up with her. It was all over in seconds and the release was unreal. Like a whirlwind had hit us.

I tried rolling off her as I softened, but she squeezed her legs together and said: "Stay there a little longer. It feels so good. What a nice way to wake up."

Shortly, my wrist-watch alarm signaled 5:30, and I had to clean up before I could go down and get coffee and breakfast. Reluctantly, I rolled off of her, climbed out of bed and headed for the shower. I knew that if we went into the shower together it would take a lot longer to get ready and we had to get to work early this morning.

CHAPTER 6

We had an intimate carry-out breakfast in our room, combined with a few kisses and a little fondling, before we headed back to the office.

As we pulled into the almost empty parking lot behind the building, I suggested that she move her car so someone wouldn't wonder how she came to park in the same spot two mornings in a row.

I parked a little ways away from her, went and unlocked the outer door and waited while Becky came in.

We walked up to the second floor together and went to her office where I gave her a very passionate kiss, while pulling her tight up against me, and said: "I'll talk to you later about plans for tonight." With that, she kissed me again and said: "I can't wait to hear what you have planned."

Then I headed into the lab.

It was the custom in the lab, that the first person in to work made the first pot of coffee. So that is what I did, before heading to my office.

I began to plot some extra-curricular activity for us for the rest of the week. Since her husband and my wife were both away for the rest of the week, we could have a lot of time together, but we needed to be careful about interaction around the office, so we didn't start any gossip. And we needed to be a little more cautious about where we went, so as to avoid being seen, by any of our close friends or acquaintances, in a compromising situation.

CHAPTER 7

The morning passed quickly. I ran off the punch cards for my test program on the computer, and Becky walked me through the process of loading the cards, making the magnetic tape, and using it to run the computer. It seemed like it would be pretty easy to run after going through all the operations, and I made some notes to help me remember key steps.

We managed to keep our contact to a minimum since there were other engineers and techs working all around the lab and the computer room had large plate glass windows as walls. We both wanted to maintain the appearance of just a working relationship, if we could.

I wanted to work through the lunch hour so Becky went out and brought in a couple of sandwiches for us.

We agreed that we needed to go to our homes after work, to check on any messages and to keep a somewhat normal routine so our neighbors didn't get curious about why we weren't home. Becky was sure that her husband would be calling after his meetings and she wanted to be home to take his call. My wife knew that I was going to be working long hours because of the new job and the pressure to meet schedules, so I wasn't expecting her to call. I did want to be able to chat across the fence with a neighbor just so things seemed normal.

We agreed to meet at the mall parking lot, after Becky got her call, and leave Becky's car there, while we went to dinner out of town. I had picked another cozy little restaurant that was in a city about 20 miles away.

CHAPTER 8

It was about 8 o'clock that evening, when we met at the mall. I was really keyed up about being with Becky again and gave her a long hug and kiss when she got in the car.

My Buick Super had bench seats, so Becky slid over next to me and didn't waste any time getting her hand on my leg and to the bulge in my pants that already had formed just in anticipation of the evening. That was almost too much for me. I thought I might blow my wad on the way to dinner, but I managed to hold myself together

On the way over, I told her that I had also made a reservation at a little roadside "no-tell-motel" for our after dinner desert. Well, Becky was so hot and bothered she suggested that we should just stop at a convenience store and pick up some snacks and drinks and skip dinner. Needless to say, that was fine with me, since she had been warming me up all the way.

I had no sooner gotten our door open at the motel, when Becky started shedding clothes. So I followed her lead and soon we were down to our shorts. When her bra came off, I couldn't keep my mouth off her nipples. They were sticking straight out like little pointers just waiting for me. After a couple of minutes of sucking and kissing, I picked her up, laid her down on the bed and proceeded to slowly pull her panties off. As I did this my mouth was busy kissing her stomach, then her cute little belly button, then down to her treasure.

After a few minutes of this she couldn't take any more and pulled me up onto the bed with her. Then she proceeded to pull my shorts off, which wasn't easy because of the giant hard-on that she had to negotiate. She dropped her mouth onto my member and within a few minutes had me good and lubricated and stiff like a flag-pole.

Sliding her body up mine she soon straddled me with her sopping pussy massaging my pole, then suddenly she drove me home up to the hilt, and there she paused. I thought she might have injured something, because she was sitting there with her eyes closed and her head up in the air. Then she started to quiver and slowly started moving up and down on me, like she was in a trance.

Then, she started moving, faster and faster, and all I could do was lie there and enjoy it. She was in full control.

I knew this wasn't going to take long, and soon she whispered: "*get ready, here I come*". I didn't need any encouragement because I was just trying to hold my load as long as I could, and I knew I was losing that battle. Then she started to quiver and shake accompanied by little moans and screams, as she orgasmed, for what seemed like 2 minutes. As I came with her I thought I must be draining all of the liquid out of my body, because my climax lasted so long too. Finally Becky slumped against me as I slipped out of her.

Exhausted, Becky rolled off me and curled up in my arms with her head on my chest. With a soft whisper she said: "I've been thinking of this all day. I wasn't sure I could get out of the computer room without creaming my jeans, while we were working today."

After we had recovered, somewhat, we had some of the snacks that we had bought, while sitting in the bed, stark naked.

Because we had gotten a late start, we decided we should get a quick shower and head home, because we still had a half hour drive.

Getting in the shower together, again, I started soaping her all over, and this was getting me aroused. As I was washing her back and got down to her butt, I couldn't keep from washing right through to her crotch. This was so erotic, for me, that I pushed her up against the wall and put my meat up into her pussy from behind and just started pumping away. I was so turned on that it only took about 30 seconds and I felt myself ready to blow. As I let her know I was coming, she responded by pushing back against me until we came together with simultaneous cries of release.

We finally managed to complete the shower, get dried off, dressed, and back out to the car.

Becky slept during most of the drive home and was surprised when we got to her car so quickly. With a long kiss goodnight, we reluctantly parted, each heading home.

CHAPTER 9
Wednesday

Wednesday passed quietly. Becky and I were both tied up in meetings most of the day, so we could only meet for a short time when we got into the office. Just time for a quick kiss and murmurs of how we were going to miss seeing each other during the day.

We agreed to meet at 6:30 at Luigi's for a cozy dinner and a little time together. Realizing that the intensity of the last two days might be clouding our judgment, we were going to go home after dinner and make like home bodies.

I'm sure some of the people in my two meetings were wondering why it was that I was smiling so much. I had a hard time keeping my mind on the business of the meeting and off the last two days with Becky. Fortunately, I was not an active participant in either of the meetings, which were both with potential vendors of components and test equipment for our instrumentation. Our junior project engineer was prepared with most of the specs and questions. They were mostly "get your feet wet" meetings for me, to begin the process of getting more involved in the overall program. It's a good thing that I didn't have to stand up and talk, either, because there were times when, as my mind wandered over Becky, that my 'little man' started "standing up" in response.

After the meetings, I stopped in my office, went through my mail, and cleaned off my desk. Then I went home for a quick clean-up there. About 6:15 I headed off for Luigi's.

When I got to Luigi's, I saw that Becky's car was already there. As I walked in the door, I also saw that she was at our 'favorite' table. Looking around, I didn't see anyone that I knew, it being mid-week, there still weren't many customers, so before I slid into the chair across from her, I leaned over and gave her a long kiss while cupping and gently squeezing one of her breasts. I know she hadn't expected that, as she got a light glow and a big smile.

Dinner was as good as it had been two nights earlier. We made small talk about our meetings, and about how fast the week was going. Also how we were going to miss each other that evening being home alone. We both had our usual two glasses of Chivas Regal on the rocks, and soon dinner was over and it was time for us to leave.

By then, it was almost 8 o'clock. Becky said that she had to stop at the office for a minute and asked if I would come by the parking lot too. The parking lot was in the back of our building, but lights hadn't been installed yet, and she said she would feel safer if I was there.

As I pulled into the parking lot behind her, I was surprised when she headed for the very back corner of the lot away from the building. As I pulled up alongside her car, she turned her lights off. Then she got out, came over to my car and slid across the seat to me. She quickly turned off my car and pushed the headlight switch off, while leaning across me. I could feel the heat coming off her, as she did all of this in about 5 seconds.

After putting us in total darkness, she turned her face to mine and gave me a long, hot kiss. Her right hand was already working on my belt buckle and then on my zipper. Having undone both of those, she slid back across the seat, hunched up a little and pulled her panties off and stuffed them in her pocket.

No question of her intent. She was on a mission and I was her target.

As I slid across the seat, I pulled my pants down around my ankles, while she scrunched up against the door. As soon as I was in position, she was up on her knees, straddling me, and without a word dropped herself down on my cock. Then she whispered in my ear: "*I told you the other night, that scotch makes me 'hot' and tonight is no exception. Give me all you've got.*"

Well, that didn't take long for either one of us. Becky was so hot and wet she turned me on just with her aggressiveness, and I was ready to blow my load almost from the moment we started. Becky took control with a little back and forth rocking and a little up and down and in less than 60 seconds she started a low moaning that grew rapidly in volume. No talk was needed. I knew exactly when she was peaking and as her orgasm hit, I shot my load as high up in her as I could get my cock. When my load hit her, I knew she felt it, because she shuddered again, like a second orgasm.

After a long kiss and a tearful hard hug, Becky climbed off as I slid back across the seat. She stuffed a tissue into her pussy, pulled her panties back on, gave me another wet, hot kiss, then went back to her car. Talk about a 'quicky'. That was it, and it was great for both of us. Becky put her car in gear, backed up quickly and headed home. As soon as I could get my pants back in place and zipped up, I followed and headed for my home.

CHAPTER 10.

I had no sooner arrived home, Wednesday evening, when the phone rang. I thought it probably was my wife calling, but it wasn't. It was Marge, our next door neighbor asking if I would mind coming over for a few minutes. I told her I would be there in about 15 minutes.

I quickly jumped in the shower, because I was sure that I had the smell of a whorehouse on me from the hot and steamy session a short time earlier. I put on a light cologne and some clean clothes, all to try to dispel any lingering odor. Then I walked across the yard and knocked on Marge's door.

Marge opened it immediately, and I could see from her red eyes that she had been crying. After thanking me for coming she offered me a drink, which I accepted after seeing that she already had one. Then we sat down in her living room.

"I really appreciate your coming over, Jerry, I didn't know who else I could talk with. I'm so upset that I didn't want to get in the car and drive anywhere."

"What's wrong?" I said. "Did something happen to Dick?" I knew that he had been out of town most of the week, too.

"Well something did 'happen' to him," said Marge. And then she began crying at which point she came over and sat next to me and started crying on my shoulder, literally. "He called me today, from Las Vegas. He said he had met someone else, and he was filing for divorce in Las Vegas. Can you believe it?" she sobbed, "He *called me* to tell me. He said he wasn't coming back and that everything here was mine."

Well, I was in shock, too. I had known Dick and Marge for several years, and I thought that they had a good marriage. It was hard to believe that this was happening.

"I can't understand why he's doing this," said Marge, "I thought we had a good marriage and I never thought he was cheating on me. I must have missed some 'signs' somewhere along the way. Did Dick ever say anything to you about another woman or about leaving me?"

"I had no idea," I said, "he never even hinted at anything like this. I'm as surprised as you are."

After several more minutes of talking, I noticed that Marge was looking very pale and woozy and she had gotten real quiet. I don't know how much she had to drink, but it probably was a lot. I probably would have been a basket case in that scenario, too. I suggested that she probably should lay down and get some sleep. She mumbled something in agreement, but when she tried to get up, she couldn't stand.

So, I went into her bedroom and brought out a pillow and blanket, helped her stretch out on the couch and covered her with the blanket. I sat around and waited for a few minutes, but she was sound asleep almost as soon as I covered her. I went around the house and turned off most of the lights, locking the door as I headed home.

As I was walking home, I began to wonder who Dick had 'found' suddenly that had triggered such an extreme action on his part.

I realized that I hadn't looked at my mail before I went over to Marge's house, so I picked that out of my mailbox on the way in. The first thing that I saw was the Express Mail envelope addressed to me and mailed from Las Vegas. Who would be sending me mail from Las Vegas? I didn't know anyone out there. Oh, wait, Dick is out there now, but why would he be mailing anything to me.

I carried the envelope into the den, where I fixed another scotch-on-the-rocks, before ripping it open. I sat down behind my desk and pulled the 'tear-strip', then pulled a multi-page letter out. Turns out it wasn't from Dick, it was from my wife, Jacky. That was the first surprise.

The second surprise was the opening statement: '*I'm sorry to tell you in this manner, but.....*' and then she went on to tell me how she had been unhappy in our marriage and how Dick had consoled her during my absences and that she and Dick had decided to 'elope' and they were getting a Vegas marriage as soon as the divorce was final. She wouldn't be coming back, and I was free to do whatever I wanted with any of her belongings. She was really sorry that she had to do it this way, but she didn't have the guts to tell me in person and then have to talk about it with me.

Now, I had known for some time that we had a problem. I had suspicions that she might be having some extra-marital activities, because when I came back from trips, she usually didn't want to have sex. And some times when I was away and tried calling home, all I got was the answering machine. Even when I was home she was very cool and remote, avoiding physical contact of any kind.

But this was really out of the blue. All this time she was having an affair with Dick, our next door neighbor, my golfing partner and bowling buddy. Wow! Now I was the one who needed another drink.

After thinking it over, while staring mindlessly at the letter, I decided that I must have had some serious suspicions, even though my mind wouldn't let me bring them to the surface. It helped explain what I was doing with Becky now. That really had surprised me, when I let it get started, and it was something that I had never considered doing before.

Then my thoughts went back to Marge, next door. Apparently she had no idea that Dick was with Jacky, or she would have said something. She and Jacky were 'best friends' How do I break this news to her? Let her read

Jacky's letter? Just blurt it out? I had to tell her somehow, tomorrow.

CHAPTER 11
Thursday

It was close to 8 o'clock when I woke up in the morning. I must have fallen asleep in my chair, then climbed the stairs to bed later. I was still fully dressed, except for my shoes, and one look in the mirror made me head for the kitchen to get some coffee started. I looked like 'death' warmed over.

Normally, I would be at the office by this time. After thinking about my work schedule, I knew that I didn't have any meetings scheduled, or any tests going on where people would be depending on me for input. My boss, George, was quite loose with work time, knowing that I often worked late and on weekends. He only wanted to know that my work was getting done in a timely manner and that we were staying on schedule with NASA on our experiment.

Remembering that I had to break the news to Marge, next door, I picked up the phone and called her. She answered after a few rings and mumbled "good morning". It was easy to tell that she hadn't been up long either. Maybe I woke her. "Good Morning, Marge." I said. "I wonder if I could come over in a half hour or so to talk with you some more?"

"I would like that." said Marge. "That will give me a little time to get cleaned up and get some coffee on. I want to apologize to you for unloading on you last night. See you in a little bit."

Oh! Little did she know.

After getting a cup of coffee, shaving and showering, and getting into some clean clothes, I headed across the yard. Marge had seen me coming and had the door open. After the customary 'friends kiss', she put a cup of coffee into my hands and we sat down in her living room.

After I explained the reason for my coming over and I showed her my letter from Jacky, Marge cried quietly for a short time. "I should have seen it coming." she said. "I had some suspicions but wouldn't let myself believe that anything was going on." "It explains a lot of Dick's activities and absences though. I really appreciate your taking the time to tell me in person and so quickly. I guess it's time to stiffen up and move forward."

"I know that you have to get to work," she continued, "and I guess that I have some work to do, starting with meeting with an attorney. Can we talk again in a couple of days?"

"Absolutely." I said. "I guess we're now a two-person support group. I'll give you a call Saturday morning."

"That sounds good." she said. "Thanks again, Jerry, and try to have a good day."

CHAPTER 12

I went straight to my office, closed the door and kept the lights off while I tried to get my mind straightened out and directed at what I needed to do during this day.

One day at a time, I had heard, when you have a major problem looking you in the face.

"How do you eat an elephant?" someone had asked. "One bite at a time." said a wise man.

After a half hour of self-contemplation, I turned on the lights and opened my door. Then I walked down the hallway to Becky's door which was open as she worked at her desk.

'Knock, knock' I rapped lightly on her open door.

"Oh, good morning Jerry." she said. " I was beginning to wonder if something had happened to you, since I hadn't heard anything."

After looking up and down the hallway to make sure no one was coming, I gave her a quick kiss and hug.

"Well, something did happen." I said. "I would rather not talk about it here, but was wondering if we could get together for dinner tonight."

"Absolutely." She replied. "I would love that. I'm beginning to look forward to our 'dinners'. How about 6 o'clock at Luigi's again?"

"That sounds great to me, too." I said. "I'm going to try to get some screen room tests done this afternoon, but I should be able to have them completed by that time. I'll meet you there. Order me a double scotch, if you get there before I do."

CHAPTER 13

The day went quickly, because I tried to immerse myself in my work to block out my marital situation. By the time I finished and had written some notes on the screen room tests, it was 6 o'clock. I closed up quickly and headed for my car.

Becky's car was there when I pulled into Luigi's parking lot. As I walked in, I saw that she had 'our table' prepared with a large drink sitting waiting for me. So I gave her a quick kiss, sat and took a long sip, before I said anything to her.

I had decided that I had to let Becky know what was going on at home, because it might have a negative impact on my behavior and performance with her, even though I didn't want it to happen. So I pulled out the letter from Jacky and slid it across the table and said: "You should probably read the first couple of paragraphs of this letter that I received last night. Then I'll tell you '*the rest of the story*'."

After Becky had gotten over the shock of the letter, I told her about Dick and Marge and how Marge had learned the 'dirty' details. I explained to Becky about my suspicions and why I thought I had allowed our lovemaking to proceed and continue, since I had never strayed before. She was very quiet and looked deep in thought for a few minutes, as she sipped her scotch.

"You may find this hard to believe, but this is the first time that I have ever strayed, in my marriage, too." Becky said. "Sure, I've been attracted to other men, before. But I've never let it get to the point where I went to bed with them. I always went home and jumped Jack's bones, or used my vibrator if he wasn't home or wasn't in the mood. I was surprised at myself, after our first night together."

"What do you think changed, that caused you to go to bed with me?" I asked.

"Well, I'm not sure," she said, "but Jack and I have been having some problems of our own. We got married on the spur of the moment after a hot night of partying, and our relationship was good for a couple of years, but it seems to me, that our marriage has been going downhill the last couple of years. Jack seems to be more interested in climbing the ladder at the University, than he is in climbing into bed with me. Some nights, when I had the 'itch', I would fall asleep, waiting for him to come home, and then when he did he would go to sleep on the couch in the den instead of coming to bed. I have felt, more and more, that he had lost interest in sex with me. I thought maybe I was too aggressive with him, but when I try waiting for him to initiate sex, nothing happens."

"I guess, your timing and your invitation to dinner were just right, and that must be why I let 'us' happen." She continued. "And I have no regrets for it. I hope that you don't have any either."

"I'm not unhappy with what we've done." I said. "I did have some qualms about it after the first night, but this letter has certainly removed any feelings of guilt that I may have had. I guess I knew, in my heart, that I was just doing what I thought Jacky was doing. And I was right."

"I know that it has been a very short time," I continued, "and a very intense relationship so far, but I have come to realize that my feelings for you are more than just lust, as I thought they were the first night. I know that my feelings run deeper than that. I would hesitate to say 'I love you', but I really believe that is what is developing within me."

I understand what you're saying," said Becky, "because I have been having some strong feelings for you, other than just the sex, and I have been doing some soul searching. I've been asking myself why I've continued this relationship, when it appeared it had no place to go but into trouble. I know that we have to continue working together and I didn't want to have to be the one to say *'enough, we have to stop; there's no future in what we are doing except for trouble'*. If we were going to break it off, I knew it would get more difficult to do the longer we carried on.

I didn't want to be seen as a home-wrecker in your marriage. I don't have any regrets any more, other than I know that I am cheating on Jack. I'm going to have to figure out how to address that issue. And that has to be totally independent of what happens between you and me."

All of this time, we had both been picking at our food, and still had some of our first drinks in front of us.

"OK," I said, "Do you want to go home and take a breather from us, or do you want me to get a room for us again." I'll be the first to admit that I could use some comforting tonight. But it's your choice. I'll respect whatever you decide to do."

"That's an easy choice," she said, "make the call for the room."

* * * LOVE * * *

CHAPTER 14

After I made the room reservation, I asked Luigi if I could buy a bottle of Chivas Regal and a small bag of ice. Luigi even threw in a couple of Chivas Regal glasses and put it all in a brown paper bag with a little padding.

The motel clerk must have remembered me because we got the same room that we had on Monday night. We were a little less frantic to get naked as we got into the room, so I made sure the door was locked and the curtains all closed, before I started to get comfortable.

First, I opened the scotch and poured some over ice in Luigi's glasses. We each took a small sip, then turned and held each other in a long embrace. We knew we were making a major move in our personal lives, even though Becky was still married. It was as if, suddenly, our relationship had changed from a hunger for sex to a hunger for a more meaningful relationship. Not that the sex wasn't important or wasn't going to continue, for the time being.

I moved from rubbing Becky's back to rubbing her butt, then sliding both hands around her butt, between her legs, lightly rubbing her crotch. After a couple of minutes of this and a few moans from Becky, I began unbuttoning her blouse, pulling it off and letting it drop to the floor. Then one hand went around her back and quickly unsnapped her bra, freeing her breasts and giving my mouth access to them. I lost no time in sucking on her nipples, each in its turn.

Since I'm good at multi-tasking, while I was sucking on her nipples, my hands were also pulling her skirt down, quickly followed by her panties. Soon she was left with only her socks on, as she had shed her shoes when we came in.

Not to be outdone, she was working at the buttons on my shirt, soon getting that off and on the floor. My belt and zipper were no match for her nimble fingers and then my pants were down around my ankles, followed quickly by my briefs. Immediately she dropped to her knees and took me in her mouth, since I was already standing at attention. I stood there, enjoying her ministrations, for a couple of minutes, then pulled her up and led her into the bathroom for a shower. I love showering with a woman. You can never tell where it will lead and it is such a personal experience. You get to run your hands over every part of your partner's body with no limitations. It is so sensual.

This time was no exception. We weren't as frenetic this night as we had been the first night, but the experience was just as enjoyable. I soaped Becky from head to toe, rinsing her as I went along, and following up with my mouth wherever there was an opportunity. I sucked her nipples again, only harder this time, with more feeling, because I was getting more excited as I progressed. Then I got to her pussy again, with the fine blond hair and the already swollen lips and I could taste her juices as I kissed and sucked my way around that juicy opening.

As I was engrossed in 'cleaning' her, she was shampooing my hair and rinsing it, then she started soaping around my head and shoulders. Reaching down, she slowly pulled me upright so she could wash the rest of me, paying special attention to my ass and my cock, which was still stiffly upright, red, and glistening, stretched to its fullest. She took her time soaping up her hands and cleaning my cock very carefully and very gently until I thought I would shoot my load. Realizing that I was beginning to peak, Becky dropped to her knees, took me in her mouth and began a slow up and down, occasionally taking time to lick the head of my cock. I had to take ahold of the towel bar to keep from falling because my knees were starting to give way. Then she picked up the pace, up and down, sometimes with a little bit of teeth, but mostly squeezing her mouth around me. Soon I yelled, "*I'm comin! Now!*" and Becky bobbed up and down faster and faster until she felt my cum flowing. Then she stopped, keeping me in her mouth, and took everything that I could shoot. I'm surprised she didn't choke, but she didn't.

I was so spent, I really had to hang on to the towel bar to keep from falling. My legs felt like rubber. Becky was still licking drops off my cock and taking my now limp dick into her mouth to try to resuscitate me, but to no avail. Finally, when I was able to stand on my own, we shut off the water and toweled each other dry.

Making our way into the bedroom, we picked up our drinks, climbed into bed and settled down in each other's arms. We were content to lie quietly and bask in the after-glow of the shower and the warmth of our bodies.

"I'm glad we came here again," I said, "I will always think of this as our special room."

"I will too," said Becky, "it has been very special to me, being able to meet you and have our relationship grow so quickly. It's almost like we were meant for each other."

"I know what you mean. It seems like events that, at first glance, seem independent have actually been pre-ordained. If you hadn't been in my life when Jacky's letter came, I probably would be a basket case right now, drunk some place. Even though I knew there was some under-current in my home life, I never saw Jacky and Dick 'eloping'. Your being here helped soften the blow and the shock of that."

"I want to always be here for you." said Becky, "I just don't know, at the moment, how I will make that happen. I know that it probably is too early to know this and to say it, but I do think that I am in love with you."

"That is a big step in our relationship, but I too have been having the same thoughts. I think that what may have started out as a basic sexual need, *lust*, for both of us has, for me, started to grow into a much deeper feeling. I don't know if I should say that 'I love you', but that is what I am beginning to feel."

"Well, I can tell that you have some 'hard' feelings for me." She replied, as her right hand started caressing my cock, which had been growing taller without my realizing it.

Not wanting to let her have all the fun, I started playing with her nipples with my left hand, then with my tongue and mouth. I let my hand wander down her smooth stomach to her soft pussy hair, where my fingers soon found a wet mound waiting to be caressed. While multi-tasking this way can be nice, I soon let my tongue and mouth trace their way down to that sopping mound and those hot, pink pussy lips. A few minutes of sucking on her clitoris was all it took to bring her to a moaning orgasm.

Not wanting to be left out of the party, I slid my body up over hers and positioned my still stiff member against her pussy and began just rubbing up and down. But Becky was so ready, she quickly moved so that she caught me and I slipped inside of her. Kissing her long and hard, with our tongues intertwining, made us both hotter and faster. Soon we were just banging away as fast and as hard as we could. Just a good old fashioned fucking. After the shower 'cleaning', I was able to control myself longer, so we went on for about 10 minutes until we both felt ourselves losing control and we came together in one final crashing orgasm.

As she felt me starting to roll off, she said, "Stay there for a little longer. I love the feel of you inside me." So I just relaxed and let my weight down gradually on her and we just hugged each other in contentment.

Before long, while still hugging each other, we rolled over on our sides and went back to long kisses. We must have both been exhausted, because the next thing I knew, looking at the clock on the nightstand, it was 5 am. We had fallen asleep entwined and were still that way when I woke up.

CHAPTER 15
Friday

Becky was still sleeping in my arms, and then I realized that while I had been asleep, my cock, somehow, had stayed inside of her and now had risen and was ready for action. Not wanting to waste a good thing, I began a slow hip movement so that I was moving up and down inside of her. I repositioned myself, slightly, so I could put a little more pressure on her clitoris and that soon had its desired effect. Without any words, Becky started moving her hips in unison with mine. As I kissed her neck and her eyelids, she opened one eye, smiled and gave me a long kiss, while keeping up her hip motion. Then, suddenly, she rolled over on top of me and began putting more pressure on her clitoris, and of course, more pressure on my cock. This was so effective that I couldn't hold myself and began filling her with cum, thrusting as high up in her as I could. When she felt my jism hit her, she jerked, and almost immediately began to shudder and spasm and she came with a loud cry of pleasure. *"OH! god! That feels so good."*

As we relaxed and she lay on top of me, she said: "Oh, I do love you Jerry. I do. I can't not say it, when I feel it so strongly."

"I love you, too, Becky. I'm so happy that you feel the same way. I've heard people talk about 'Love at first sight', but I never believed it until now. Now we have to figure out what to do about it."

CHAPTER 16

Even though we got to the office early, the day went very quickly. We both did our best to stay busy, so as not to think too much about what was or wasn't going to happen.

We had talked about our possible future at breakfast, but we didn't reach any conclusions. Though Becky's husband, Jack, was going to be home that evening, we knew that we had to be able to get together sometime over the weekend.

I went out at noon and bought a couple of sandwiches for us, which we ate in the coffee room.

While we were eating, I suggested that we meet at a small, secluded parking lot on a nearby lake on Sunday. It was mushroom season and there were mushrooms up in the woods around the lake. It was a location that not a lot of people knew, so we had a good chance of having some privacy. Becky readily agreed to that as it gave her an excuse to get out, and since Jack wasn't the outdoorsy type so he wouldn't insist on going with her.

With that decided, we finished lunch and left the coffee room, each of us heading in different directions to our offices. The engineers' offices each had two entrances, one into the lab, and the other into the main hallway. So I went into my office from the lab and right from it into the hallway and walked down to Becky's office. She was expecting me and closed her door as soon as I entered. We knew we only had a few minutes before we needed to be back at work, so a long hug and a longer kiss was all we had time for.

"I'm really going to miss being with you tonight." said Becky. "I'm so hungry for your touch and for you 'loving'. It's going to drive me crazy having to wait until Sunday to be with you."

"I'm hoping that Jack gets home early enough that he and I can have a discussion about our relationship. I have a feeling that he is ready for a serious appraisal and a solution. And it couldn't come at a better time."

"I hope that you can be patient with me, for a little bit." she continued, "I really do love you and want to be with you."

"I'll wait." I said. "I have plenty to keep me busy, and I know what the 'pot-of-gold' is at the end of the rainbow."

"I also have to call an attorney friend and make sure that I think of everything that I have to do in my own situation."

"Then there's Marge, next door. I promised her I would get together with her on Saturday and help keep her on an even keel. I don't want to see her turn into a basket case because of my wife running off with her husband. I feel guilty that I'm partly responsible for that happening."

"I'd better get back to the lab, now. I'll see you on Sunday, at 1 o'clock at the lake. OK?"

"I'll be there, with my mushroom bags. It's going to be painful waiting that long, but

I'm sure you can make it worthwhile." she said, with a big smile.

I gave her another hug and kiss and then went back upstairs to the screen room to get some work done.

It was eerily quiet in the screen room, because in addition to the copper screening, it also had acoustic padding on all six sides. Not many people came up here unless they had tests that they had to run on satellite instrumentation and, at the moment, I was the only one with instrumentation that was ready for these kinds of tests.

And suddenly, I thought of another valuable experiment to try out in this room, someday soon.

CHAPTER 17
Weekend

Saturday passed quickly. Marge even seemed somewhat upbeat about her situation. She had met with an attorney and said that everything was under control. She was planning on selling the house and moving back to her hometown in Virginia.

I spent most of the day making a list of Jacky's 'things' that I wanted to get rid of quickly, most of them probably going to Goodwill. As I did this, I was thinking 'good riddance'.

Sunday dawned with a clear sky and a forecast of temps in the high 60s, which was good enough for an afternoon in the woods. I packed a lunch basket, adding a bottle of Robert Mondavi wine, and then pulled an old Marine Corps blanket from the closet.

I drove out to the lake a bit early, partly because I was so eager to see Becky again, and partly because I wanted to scope out the parking lot and see if we were going to have any 'company' in the area. The parking lot was empty when I got there, which was good to see. So I shut off the car, leaned back in the seat and closed my eyes. It had been a hectic week and I had missed some sleep along the way.

I was awakened by the sound of another car pulling in, and when I opened my eyes I was glad to see that it was Becky, alone. Grabbing the blanket and basket, I got out, locked the car, and went to greet her. When she got out of her car, I actually grabbed her and hugged her to me, I was so eager to see her again.

"I missed you, so much, my love." I said, at which point the bulge in the front of my pants was pressing into her crotch, reinforcing my words.

"I missed you, too," said Becky, "and I've been on the verge of creaming my jeans on the drive over here, just thinking about spending the afternoon with you."

Heading up into the woods, we soon found a clump of small fir trees surrounding a nice mossy patch. This provided a secluded setting where we were almost completely hidden by view from the rest of the woods. As I spread the blanket and set the basket down, Becky came up behind me, putting her arms around me while her hands groped me and started working on my zipper.

While she was working on my zipper, I reached around and started working on the buttons on her jeans. Then turning around, I said: "Stand still, let me take care of these." And with that I dropped my pants and stepped out of them, then returned to her buttons and soon had her jeans down around her ankles.

Dropping to my knees, and pulling her panties down at the same time, I put my mouth and tongue to her sopping wet pussy. But she couldn't stand it, almost literally. She dropped to her knees and quickly pulled her jeans and panties off her feet. Lying down on the blanket, she said: "I just can't wait. I am so hot. I need you inside me, now."

Since I was bursting my shorts, I tore them off, and got down on top of her. As I began rubbing my cock up and down along her legs, she cried out: "*No*, I really mean it, I want you inside me *now*. I don't need any foreplay."

Plunging my hot, swollen cock home as deeply as I could, I felt an immediate shudder from Becky. She was having an instant orgasm. She squeezed her pussy around my cock so hard that it provided the instant stimulation for me, and I started franticly thrusting in and out and within seconds I came in a burst of hot cum which caused Becky to shudder again with another orgasm. As her shuddering started to subside, I let myself down on her, while my cock stayed half erect still inside her.

"Oh my god," she said, "I have wanted this so much. I've missed you so much, Two days has seemed like an eternity."

"I'm sure you can tell how much I've missed you, too." I said. "I can usually hold out longer than I did, but it is wonderful being back with you. It feels so good being inside of you like this."

"Well," she said, "I may have some good news too. Jack and I spent most of Saturday talking about our current monastic life-style, and we agreed to go our separate ways. He admitted that the luster had worn off of our relationship. He said he really wasn't as sexually charged as I was, and that had caused him to spend more time at work and to avoid me as much as he could. He admitted that he really wanted to be able to concentrate on advancing his career."

"We have agreed to part and get a no-fault divorce. We are going to move into separate apartments as soon as we can make the arrangements."

"I believe that this was inevitable, with or without you in the picture. It's just that your being in my life, which he doesn't know about yet, has provided the impetus to make it happen. And I couldn't be happier."

"That is great news, for me." I said. "I hope that it is for you too. I'm sure that parting, even after the few years you were together, is difficult. You must have had some strong feelings for Jack at one time. I'll be there for you, if you need someone to lean on, anytime, anyplace."

As we were talking, I could feel myself rising again inside of her, and I knew she could feel it too. She was making some very slight adjustments in our sandwiched bodies.

Without warning, she wrapped her arms tighter about me and rolled me over so she was on top.

"My turn," she said. "lie back and let me do my thing. I want more time to enjoy this one"

With that she started, first squeezing her pussy together around my cock, then slowly, with short movements, sliding up and down, getting her clitoris exactly where she wanted it while at the same time giving me good stimulation.

I just closed my eyes, enjoying the sensation, while my hands gently rubbed her back and her ass, squeezing her cheeks, gently once in a while, and occasionally probing her ass with a finger.

After a few minutes of this gentle, slow love making, she stopped, leaned over and whispered in my ear. "I want us to try something new. I used an enema just before coming out here and I want you to take me in the ass. Is that all right with you?"

"I have to admit," I replied, "it is something I've never done, but it sounds interesting to me. You know what they say: 'Any port in a storm.'"

With that, Becky rolled off me, got down on her hands and knees in front of me and wiggled her ass at me.

I didn't need a second invitation, still being 'up', hard as a rock, and well lubricated.

"Tell me if it hurts, too much, or gets really uncomfortable." I said.

"OK" she replied, as I got on my knees behind her with my cock at the 'door'. Gently entering her, with my hands on her waist, I eased in slowly, trying to be gentle.

"*Oh! Yes! Oh, that feels so good, Ohhh.*" Becky moaned and sighed as I got deep inside of her, but she was also pushing back on me, trying to get me in deeper.

When my balls hit her ass, I knew I was in as far as I was going to go, so I started a gentle in and out motion, while one of my hands was busy rubbing her clit and the other was massaging a tit. Talk about being fully involved. This was it.

Not to be outdone, one of Becky's hands was massaging my balls, giving me encouragement.

"*OH*," she cried excitedly. "this is so erotic. I have to tell you, now, I have never done this before, either. I have read about it, but never had the desire to experience it until I met you. I want, so much, for us to be as one, and I thought this was the time to try this."

"*OH god,*" she cried again, as she started to shudder and shake. "It's like an earthquake coming. Don't stop, just fill me with everything you have."

Hearing those words and feeling her body quivering spasmodically, I felt myself coming too. In a final couple of thrusts, we both went over the edge, violently climaxing together, then collapsing on the blanket, exhausted.

After I recovered my senses, a little, I pulled the blanket over us and we took a nap for about an hour. Then, after getting dressed, we decided to really hunt for some mushrooms. We both liked the morels, which were supposed to be at their peak now. We found an area where there were quite a few of them, so we filled two of Becky's bags, one for her and one for me.

As we made our way back to the cars, we were holding hands and swinging our arms like two kids who just had a fun time, which we certainly had.

"This has been a wonderful afternoon." I said, as we approached the cars. "I have to fly to California tomorrow for a series of meetings on the interface between the experiment and the satellite. I won't be back until late Wednesday, so I'll see you on Thursday."

"I'm going to miss you terribly while I'm gone," I continued. "but you've given me a lot to help keep my spirits up while we're apart."

"Oh, I'm devastated!" she replied. *"Just kidding!"* But it will be so lonely without you. I guess I'll just have to think about our outing this afternoon and what a great time it was. I'll be in early on Thursday in case you can be too."

"Well, I do have a special surprise planned for you on Thursday, and all I can tell you is that you won't have to travel far to enjoy it."

"Oh, you're a '*meany*', can you give me a little clue?"

"Well, let's see, what can I tell you? It is indoors, it's not far away, and you may have to do some improvisation. But that's all I can tell you."

"OK, I guess that will give my imagination something to work on. Please have a safe trip, and hurry home to me."

WEEK TWO

We both got into the office early on Thursday and met in Becky's office for a quick hug and a kiss.

"Oh, I'm so glad you're back, I've missed you so much. I hope you won't have to travel too much."

"I've been going out of my mind trying to figure out what and where your surprise could be. Can you tell me now?"

"Not yet. Let's wait until this afternoon after I get my report done on the California meetings. If you'll get us some sandwiches for lunch, I'll give you another clue."

Then it was back to work. Becky to her computer and me to my office.

Becky went out at noon and brought sandwiches for us.

"All right, enough suspense," she said, "what is the next clue?"

"When you get a little free time," I said, "why don't you come up the back stairs to the screen room?"

"Oh, is there something up there for me to see?" she inquired.

"I'll be there." I said, "Isn't that enough?"

"Will anyone else be there?" she asked.

"No, just you and me."

"*Oh*," she softly squealed, "I think I'm beginning to like where this is heading. I'll be discreet, when I come up there."

"That would be a good idea." I said, "Discretion *is* the better part of sin."

CHAPTER 19

About 2 o'clock, as I was running some tests in the screen room, there came a tap, tap at the door. I had to go open it, because it needs to be kept sealed during experiment tests.

"I've come to see what kind of surprise has *come up*." said Becky, as I relocked the door. "I hope it's going to be worth the climb up the stairs."

"I think you're going to like it," I said, as I took her in my arms and started kissing her, taking care not to leave 'strawberry' marks on her throat.

At the same time, my hands started to slide her skirt down, taking her panties along with it.

"*Oh, my* !" she squealed breathlessly, "*Whatever are you doing*?"

At the same time, I felt one of her hands going to work on the bulge in the front of my pants and the other going to work on my belt and zipper. Soon we were both standing there with our clothes down around our ankles, kissing passionately

I walked backwards, pulling her with me, to a raised stool that I had already placed in position for this event. Sitting back on the stool, I gently pulled her towards me, so that she had to spread her legs around mine. Placing both feet up on the side rungs, she discovered she was in the perfect position to lower herself on my straining cock and engulf it, which she did with a soft moan. Sitting on my lap with my tool throbbing in her, she sighed and gave me a very wet kiss.

"I could never have imagined this." she said, "This is exciting and it feels so good again. But it would seem that I am going to have to do most of the work here, because I have you pinned to this stool. How does this feel?" as she raised herself slightly and then relaxed back down.

"Heavenly," I said, "I'll help out however I can, but I can feel that I'm not going to take long to come, so do what feels best for you. I want you to enjoy this as much as I'm going to."

I tried raising and lowering my legs, slightly, to help with the action, but soon realized that I was not staying in contact with her clit, so I stopped and let her do all the moving. She was rotating her ass, sort of back and forth and side to side, keeping her clit in close contact with my cock. This resulted in both of us peaking at the same time, with me shooting my load and her orgasm.

As her body quit spasming, she moaned: "*Oh, what a great welcome home party*. I never would have believed we could do this here. I'm sure glad that this door locks from the inside. I'm also glad the room is sound insulated. If it hadn't been, the whole building would have heard me cry out when I came."

CHAPTER 20

We were sitting in the coffee room on Friday, talking quietly.

"Before we had met," I said, "I had put in for a weeks' vacation, starting in two weeks. I had been thinking of taking a trip out to Colorado to see Rocky Mountain National Park and a few other places that I've never seen. Is there any chance you could get away too?"

"If you can't get away," I continued: "I'm going to cancel my vacation, until we can go somewhere together."

"I think that timing sounds perfect," said Becky, "Jack has rented another apartment and he is going to be moving out in a couple of weeks. I would rather not be around when he does. Let me talk to my boss and see if I can get the time off."

"Good," I said, "As soon as you find out you can go, I will make the plane reservations. I have been told we won't need hotel reservations because it is so early in the season, most places are eager to have any customers. So we'll probably have a good pick of where we want to stay plus the freedom to move around as we want."

"On another note, I have been told by some of the other engineers, that I have been a party pooper by not showing up for the TGIF parties. How about both of us going tonight after work? It's over on my side of town at a place called 'Georgie's', that has 2 for 1 prices on Friday evening."

"Sounds great, I would enjoy that." said Becky. "I'll park my car in the mall parking lot, if you'll pick me up there. Then I won't have far to drive home after the party."

"Works for me. I'll pick you up about 5:30. It'll do us good to mingle more with the crew around here. And I hear that they have a real good time, too."

There was a good turnout at Georgie's and it sounded like the party had started without us. There were loud shouts as we came in and found places to sit. In addition to the men, there were three other females there, one secretary and a couple of female engineers. Becky spent some time talking with the girls while I did some story telling with the guys.

As the party settled down a bit, Becky and I managed to find chairs together at a large table. Soon, her free hand, hidden by the table, found my crotch and began massaging and squeezing my family jewels, causing me to have some difficulty carrying on a coherent discussion.

I had almost forgotten how turned on Becky got with a couple of glasses of scotch. And as I learned, she had had four drinks, two paid and two free, while I had nursed my two drinks along. We did have some shrimp and other h'orderves early on so we weren't drinking on empty stomachs.

Making our apologies to the gang, which by this time was smaller, we started back into town.

As we passed a cemetery on the right, Becky suddenly said: "Pull into here."

Obediently I turned onto one of the roads that wound through the cemetery, leading us to the back. I was thinking, 'Maybe she needs to pee.'

Then she said. "Pull over here." Once we were stopped, she reached over and turned the key off. At the same time she began working on my belt buckle and my zipper.

No sooner had she gotten those open, she slid over on her side and patted the seat beside her.

"Slide over here," she said, "I can't go home like this. I'm too hot and bothered. I want you here and now. And I don't care if we're seen."

"I'm your humble servant." I mocked, as I slid my pants down around my ankles and slid across the seat.

I hadn't noticed that she already had her panties off and her skirt hiked up, but she was sitting astride me before I could get settled. Luckily, my cock had anticipated just such an event and had risen to the occasion by itself.

94

"*You know my problem with scotch*." she whispered in my ear, as she started doing the rhumba in my lap. "Isn't that why you kept my drinks replenished?"

And she was right, I had tried my best to see that she didn't have an empty glass in her hand for long. It *must have been* a contrivance on my part, knowing that it would lead to something like this.

So I just sat back and enjoyed her lap dance which very shortly led to both of us losing control and moaning to each other: "*Oh, now, now, hurry, hurry, I'm coming now*!" I could feel her juice and mine running down my legs, as she sagged against me, totally spent. I didn't realize until later that I was going to have to wash the seats over the weekend.

WEEK THREE

CHAPTER 21

Sunday morning as I was enjoying my first cup of coffee, I was surprised to hear a car door close in the driveway. Looking out, I saw it was Becky

As I opened the door for her she waved a bag of bagels at me along with the Sunday New York Times.

"I couldn't stay away." she said. "I hope you don't mind me coming here."

"You can '*come*' here anytime you want." I said with a smirk. "*Me casa, su casa.*" while giving her a kiss and a squeeze of her ass.

"Can I spend most of the day here?" she asked. "My place is so quiet and I miss being with you."

"You can stay as long as you like. I have plenty of food, something to drink and a nice fireplace to keep us warm. We can have some more coffee and bagels. Then I'll light a fire and we can lie in front of the fireplace and work the Times crossword puzzle together."

"That sounds heavenly. Start me off with a cup of coffee, light cream, no sugar."

"I've been using Jamaican Blue Mountain coffee," I said, "It is hard to come by, but I have a friend who keeps me supplied. It is a rich, dark coffee, with a very slight hint of rum flavoring."

"OK, but I need some of your sugar before the coffee, Hold me and hug me and kiss me. Tell me that you will never let me go. I'm feeling depressed because we have to spend so much time apart."

"Babe," I said, "I promise, I will never let you go. I think we should use the trip to Colorado, if you can get time off, as sort of a pre-honeymoon. I know that it is going to be quite a while before we both are legally free from our spouses, but I don't want that to keep us apart any longer than necessary.

"*Oh*, you know exactly what to say, to make me feel better." she said. At the same time she had a hand inside my shorts, fondling me and raising my manhood. Not to be outdone, I had raised her skirt with one hand and was busy inside of her panties.

Leading her into the living room, I laid her down on the sofa and straddled her slim, sleek body. God, she had a gorgeous body. As I said before, her breasts weren't big, but they were so well formed with nice pert nipples. Oh, did I forget to mention that she had pulled off her sweater and blouse on the way into the living room?

Placing my cock at the entrance to her honey hole, I gently proceeded to enter her while lightly pinching one of her nipples and passionately kissing her. She responded by grasping my buttocks with her hands trying to pull me in deeper, while moaning and sighing with the pleasure it was bringing her. We proceeded slowly, enjoying the feelings we were experiencing, knowing that there was no rush. Much later, it seemed, we came gently and quietly, each recognizing that the other was coming too.

As I turned on my side, I kissed her some more, not caring if I left 'strawberry' marks on her neck or not.

"This is so good," I said, "and what a nice surprise." as I gently caressed her body running my hands up and down from her buttocks to her head, trying to learn, by feel, every part of her.

The rest of the day seemed to follow this 'easy' pattern. After coffee with bagels and cream cheese, I started a fire in the fireplace and we spread out in front of it to read the Times. Then we worked the crossword puzzle, taking turns at reading the clues.

Later we curled up on the love-seat to watch an old movie, with Becky curled up in my arms, crying at some of the poignant moments. She was such a softie, and I loved it.

Becky insisted on showing me her culinary skills as the day waned. She fixed a light dinner of shrimp and scallops in a white sauce with noodles, and we christened the meal with a bottle of Robert Mondavi Chardonnay.

Since Becky had done the cooking, I wouldn't let her do the dishes, but I insisted on rewarding her for her excellent meal.

Since we were, again, sitting on the floor in front of the fireplace, I gently laid her down, pulling off the bathrobe that she had donned earlier. After a few kisses up and down her body, she pulled me down on top of her, putting my now erect penis in where it belonged, and began a slow dance with her hips to the music of Scheherazade.

Well, let me tell you, that didn't take me long to shoot my jiz, which in turn caused Becky to have a gentle orgasm too. Afterwards we just lay there watching the fire flicker, until she decided she would head for home. I couldn't talk her into staying the night. She had clothes to prepare for work the next day, and she was feeling a little self-conscious about sleeping over at my house so soon after my wife, Jacky, had left it.

After locating most of her clothes and getting decently dressed, we walked out to her car for a final kiss and hug before she drove away.

CHAPTER 22

Late Monday morning, Becky came by and told me that her boss had approved her request for vacation time, which was great news.

After she left, I got on the phone to United Air Lines and made our round-trip flight reservations to Denver. I had already reserved a cabin in Rocky Mountain National Park for a few days. I had planned on driving around and stopping wherever I found myself, so I hadn't made any other overnight reservations. I also had a car reserved, so we were pretty well set for the trip.

It seemed like the week passed so quickly. We both had work to get wrapped up and meetings with people who were going to cover for us while we were gone, so we didn't get to see each other very much. We did manage to get in a couple of 'quickies' up in the screen room, but they only made us miss each other more.

We had made plans to get together on Saturday and drive to a political rally for an aspiring Democratic Presidential candidate that Becky liked. I was a staunch Republican, but I agreed to go with her in order to get more time together, and also because the weather wasn't looking great and she was concerned about driving over by herself.

The rally was interesting, but the candidate was wishy-washy and a bit of a fop, so neither one of us was too impressed with him.

As we walked out of the rally, we were greeted with a late winter snow that already was coming down heavily. I still had good winter mud-snow tires on my car, so I wasn't too worried. I was more concerned about the way other people handled it. We had a 50 mile drive, mostly on an Interstate highway, and the road wasn't in the best of condition. About halfway home, after driving slowly for an hour, we pulled into a restaurant for a pit stop and a cup of coffee. I suggested that we might want to stay over at a nearby motel until morning, but Becky wanted.to continue, so we got back on the road. After another hour of slow driving, we made it back to Becky's apartment. Pulling up to the curb, I put the car in park and breathed a sigh of relief at getting back in one piece.

Becky slid over beside me and whispered in my ear: "*Let me get rid of some of that tension in you. I know you are all keyed up from the drive*." With that she began massaging the front of my pants, then, not being able to get enough contact with her 'prey', she pulled down my zipper and put her hand in my pants to get at her objective, my cock. That had the desired effect because, as soon as she freed it from its confines, it stood at attention.

Well, I was starting to get worried because we were sitting on a public street in front of houses and apartments, but then I glanced around at the windows and saw that they were already steamed up from our hot breathing. So I turned the car off, so as not to attract attention.

By then I was getting 'in the mood' and decided to get with the program. So I slid my hand under Becky's skirt, up along her leg and under the edge of her panties, which were already getting wet. I only had time to slide a couple of fingers into her twat, when she suddenly put both hands around her panties and slid them off. In one motion, I undid my belt buckle and slid my pants down around my ankles, and slid the car seat back as far as it would go. Without warning Becky rolled over onto my lap and settled herself down on my erection with an audible sigh. With a long kiss we began the front-seat dance with no music except the rhythm of our ever faster breathing. In just moments we both reached a mind altering climax.

After a minute of gentle kissing and hugging, Becky rolled back to her side of the seat, stuffed her panties into her pocket, gave me a quick kiss and left the car. It took me a couple of minutes to rearrange my clothes and get the car seat in position for driving. Then realizing that I couldn't see out of the windows because of the steam, I had to take out my handkerchief and clean off the inside of the windshield. Putting the hot air blower on high helped, so I could see to drive home.

The following week went by in a flash, it seemed. Before I knew it, it was Saturday morning and time to head for the airport. Becky was taking her car into a repair garage for some work and they were going to keep it for her while she was gone. As soon as I pulled up to the garage, she threw her bag into the car and we headed to the airport.

WEEK FOUR

COLORADO

LOVE

CHAPTER 23

When we settled into our seats on the plane, we were finally able to relax. As our flight leveled out we had a light meal and a glass of wine and toasted our first trip together. Then we settled back and took a short nap.

I had scheduled the trip for this time of year, because the ski season was over and it was too early for summer vacationers. I figured that would let us travel around and see the most unspoiled scenery while not having to contend with tourists and room reservations. It wouldn't hurt that prices might be better this time of year as well.

Landing in Denver, we got our rental car and drove out to the north side of Denver where we picked out a clean looking motel and checked in. After a light dinner and one drink, we went back to the motel, took a water-saving shower together, with only a little hanky-panky and settled down on the bed to watch the news and an old movie.

Only later realizing we had fallen asleep with the TV on.

Waking up in the morning, I found myself with my usual morning erection. Not wanting to waste it, I began sliding my hand gently up and down Becky's bare body, from her pert hard nipples to the soft, fine hair of her pussy. As I felt her responding, I increased my time at her pussy, finally inserting one and then two fingers to fondle her clit. Once I felt her juices start to flow, I lowered my head and let my tongue and lips take the place of my fingers. Becky soon took me by the ears and pulled me up on top of her, so that I could put my hard-on to better use. A slow gentle movement soon produced a quiet, gentle climax for both of us. What a nice way to wake up.

We packed our bags, checked out, got a simple breakfast of bagels and coffee and were on the road early, heading for Estes Park and home for the next few days.

On arrival at Estes Park we found the cabins, where I had the reservations. We were the only customers scheduled for the week, so we got our choice and picked the one with the best view.   Now began our 'experiment' in living and making decisions together. We wanted to see how we would get along on a more intimate daily basis.

We went to a nearby grocery and picked out a variety of meats, groceries, and snacks to last us for three days. We were going to cook and eat most of our meals in.

Then we took our first drive into Rocky Mountain National Park, buying a weekly permit, since we wanted to explore as much as we could.

On impulse, while we were at the store, I had bought a collapsible fly fishing rod and a kit of flys, thinking that I might be able to get in a little fishing. When we checked in at the Park office, I was able to buy a weekly fishing permit, too.

Driving around and exploring the deserted Park, we were able to see a lot of deer, a few elk, and even a momma black bear with a couple of cubs. The woods, lakes, and the snow-capped mountains were spectacular by themselves, along with the numerous streams that we crossed. We stopped for a late lunch alongside a stream with a large grassy bank and ate sandwiches that we had made from our grocery purchases. After lunch we scouted around to find what looked like it might be a good place to try some fly fishing the next day. Then, because of the mountains towering around us, we could tell it was going to get dark early, so we headed back to our cabin.

"Let's grill hamburgers and make a salad for dinner." Said Becky.

"Works for me, I'll get the charcoal going in the grill as soon as we get back. You take care of the salad and I'll cook some perfect burgers. How do you want yours done?"

"Deal." She said. "I like mine medium rare, pink but no blood. Do you want onions on your salad?"

"Only if you eat them too." I said. "I don't want any excuses for not being able to kiss you. I like onions on my hamburger, too."

After a relaxing dinner with a bottle of cheap red wine we cleaned the dishes together, then went outside and sat on the porch to watch the sun go down over the mountains. It started to cool down quickly after that, so we went back inside, where I pulled out a book to read.

"Well, if you're going to read, I'm going to knit." Said Becky. "I'm making a sweater for a friend and I need to get it finished soon."

After a couple of hours, I put the book down and went to shave, shower and brush my teeth. When I was finished, Becky took over the bathroom and I climbed into bed with my book to wait for her to finish.

"I'm done, would you dry my back? It's a little cool and I don't want to catch a cold."

With that she tossed me the towel and stood there bare-ass naked for me to admire her. Which I did with great pleasure, because she was so hot to look at. As she sat down on the bed, I began toweling off her back. Finishing that, I moved the towel around to her breasts, making sure that I got each one good and dry, then I moved the towel down to her thighs. Then I tossed it aside and just used my hands.

"If you keep that up, you better get something else up." She said.

"Not to worry. It's already up and ready for action." I replied, pulling her down on the bed alongside me.

Rolling over on top of her, I showed her how ready I was by sliding my magic wand into her honey hole as far as I could go.

"*Oh! I can feel that*! You seem extra-long tonight. Have you been exercising it, or are you just happy to be with me."

"I'm just really happy to be out here with just you around. The only exercise it has been getting is from you, and you have been keeping it busy, haven't you?"

"I try. But how about less talk and more action at the moment. I feel like I'm about ready to explode and you're just lying there talking. Get busy, quickly, please."

And I did, and we both 'exploded' in just a few minutes.

"*Oh! my! That was interesting.*" She said. "I guess this mountain air must be an aphrodisiac. I didn't expect such a quick orgasm. Not complaining, you know, just surprised. And you seemed harder than usual, if that's possible."

"Well, I guess we'll just have to keep experimenting." I said. "It's not like we have anything better to do."

"By the way, other than exploring around this side of the park, what else do you want to see while we're out here?" I asked. "I saw a sign today that said the pass over the mountains is still blocked with snow, so we can't drive to the other side of the Park, that way, as we had planned."

"Well, I would like to see what the other side looks like." She said. "And I would like to see a couple of the ski resorts, like Aspen and Vail, if possible."

"I agree. I would like to see them, too."
I replied. "That means we'll have to go back
out of the mountains and probably head down
south to find another road back into the
mountains that way. Maybe we can go by
Pike's Peak while we're at it."

"Let's look at a map in the morning," I
continued. "and see how we can get there,
then work out a timetable for all that driving.
We need to be back in Denver at the airport
by Saturday night."

"OK. Sounds like a plan. But right now
just cuddle me and whisper sweet things in
my ear." She said. "I think I'm exhausted and
I'll be asleep shortly."

Sleeping in would have been nice, but,
as usual, I woke up with 'morning wood'.
Not wanting to waste it, and still in the
cuddling 'spoon' position, I gently raised
Becky's leg and slid my 'meat' into her
honey hole from behind. Becky just gave a
little moan of pleasure and let me have my
way with her. After a few minutes of fucking
this way, I rolled both of us over so Becky

was on her stomach and I was lying on her butt, still inside her and pumping away faster than ever. I had one hand massaging her clit since my prick wasn't making good contact and before long we both started to feel an urgency. My prick was so hard it felt like a metal rod, but I could feel the heat of her pussy and suddenly we came together with Becky shouting "*Oh god, don't stop, don't stop, I'm coming.*"

Moments later, I collapsed on her back, kissing her neck and shoulders while she was squeezing her pussy to try to keep me inside a little longer. In this position, it didn't work though, and I slipped out, all sticky and gooey. As I rolled over onto my back, Becky turned so she could take me in her mouth, cleaning me and gently nibbling on my penis.

"What a glorious way to wake up," said Becky. "Have I told you lately that I love you, because I do. I really do."

"Sweetheart," I said. "I love you so much that I wonder sometimes if this is real or just a dream, and I'll wake up and it will all be gone and you will be gone."

Laying her hand on my heart, she said: "Trust me, it's not a dream. I have never felt this way about any other man. I swear to you that I do love you and I always will."

CHAPTER 24
Monday

I fixed eggs, toast, and coffee for breakfast. We packed a lunch of sandwiches, chips and fruit drinks. Then we got cleaned up and went out for another scenic drive through the park. There was almost an endless assortment of roads and paths.

We ended up in the late morning at the Bear Lake area, where we hiked a bit, then went back to the car for the picnic lunch, and sat by the lake eating and enjoying the quiet and the spectacular scenery around us.

"Let's see if we can find the stream that we saw yesterday. The one that looked like it might be a good fishing spot. I'd like to see if I can catch a couple of trout for our dinner."

"OK! I brought my knitting with me, and I'll work on that while you fish."

Soon we had located our spot, parked the car and I got busy putting my fly rod together and running the line out through the guides. Then I picked out a colorful fly and fastened it on the end of the line, and I was all set.

After a couple of hours of fishing, I had two nice rainbow trout. Just enough for the two of us for dinner. It had been very enjoyable and relaxing to walk up and down the stream looking for pools that might hide the fish. I actually caught more than the two that I kept, but they were generally smaller, so I practiced 'catch and release' on them.

By mid-afternoon we started to get a few snowflakes, even though the temperature was over 50 degrees. So we packed up the car and headed back to the cabin.

Laying the Colorado map out on the table, we began to look at the possible ways to get back into the ski resorts. The best route, considering that we also wanted to stop at Pike's Peak, was to go back out to the Interstate, take it down to Colorado Springs, and then head west on US-24. We could probably stay in the city of Woodland Park overnight, which was close to Pike's Peak.

Then we could head west on US-24 to visit Aspen and Vail.

With all we wanted to see, and the amount of driving, we decided to head south the next morning, so we would have time to go up Pike's Peak on Tuesday.

With the rest of our trip planned, Becky started cutting up some baby red potatoes to go with the trout, along with some asparagus in Hollandaise sauce. I cleaned the trout, seasoned them with some lemon and salt & pepper, wrapped them in foil and put them on the grill.

While dinner was cooking, I opened a bottle of Chardonnay and we sat on the porch sipping wine and going over what we had seen in the Park.

After dinner, while Becky cleaned up the kitchen, I walked over to the office to let them know we would be leaving in the morning and paid our bill.

The shower stall was a little tight for the two of us, but we managed to squeeze in. We had really started to look forward to showering together. There is something very erotic about being able to spread soap suds everywhere on your lover's body while your fingers probe and massage all of the crooks, crannies and protrusions. This night was no different.

Becky started on me by soaping and rinsing all of my upper body. Then she took the shampoo to my hair and gave that a good cleaning. Then to my surprise, she kneeled with the shampoo and began cleaning my butt, giving me a little 'gotcha' to my anus. Then she moved around to my crotch, shampooing my hair and my penis, which by now was already erect, gently working the shampoo up and down the full length, then around my balls, finally letting the shower rinse me off. Her finishing touch was to take me in her mouth and give me a few deep throat strokes, before standing up again.

At this point, I was having some trouble standing, but obediently took the soap and began on her upper body, paying particular attention to her boobs and her hard nipples, rinsing them with the shower, then sampling them with my mouth while nibbling with my teeth.

Following Becky's lead, I shampooed her hair and rinsed it, then knelt down and began spreading the shampoo around, first to her cute little butt, making sure that I ran a finger up inside, which made her arch her back in pleasure. Then I moved around to her honey pot, lathering up the shampoo while spreading it around, rubbing up and down along her pussy, finally inserting one, then two fingers inside to get her juices flowing more.

After letting the shower rinse her, I gently sucked her pussy lips, while my tongue worked on her clit, feeling her back arch more, as she took my head in her hands and guided me.

After I stood up, I turned her towards the wall and entered her now flowing pussy with my straining, rock-hard, red-topped cock. Wrapping my arms about her and holding onto her tits, I pushed as deep as I could, then just banged away, because we were both primed and ready to blow.

"*OH!, OH!, that feels so good. OH!, OH!, yes, more, faster, harder. YES!, YES!, YES! Oh god it's so good.*"

As I shot my load, Becky had a room-shaking orgasm, that seemed to go on forever. Soon we were both spent and unable to move, like we were rooted to the spot.

Slowly, I pulled my limp cock from between her legs, where she had grasped it as it started sliding out of her. Reaching back and grasping a towel, I began to dry her off, while my legs were still wobbly. She repaid the favor afterwards, and we gingerly stepped out of the shower.

We held onto each other while we headed for the bed, where we collapsed, too exhausted even to climb under the sheets.

"At this rate, you are going to make me an old man before I reach 30." I said. "Not that I'm complaining. I have never had this much sex in such a short time, and had never dreamed that I could be 'up' for this much so quickly. You certainly have brought out the best in me."

"I'm glad that you are able to perform, and that you are happy about it. I think you're a real stud." Said Becky. "It is, of course, easier for a woman to have sex more often than it is for a man, but I have to tell you that it's exhausting for me too."

"I have never dreamed, even, of doing it this often." She continued. "And I'm not complaining either. I know that this frequency won't last, but I'm going to enjoy it as long as it does. I hope you will never get tired of making love to me."

"Not to worry, I won't get tired of making love to you." I said. "But I'll be on crutches in a couple of years if we continue at this pace."

"I don't need it this often, but I do want it to be an expression of love whenever we do make love." I continued. "Because I do love you, and I will try to respond whenever you need me."

"Right now I need some sleep," said Becky. "Just pull the sheets up over us and hold me like you did last night. I feel so protected and loved that way."

CHAPTER 25
Tuesday

It didn't take long to pack the car in the morning and we got underway before the sun was too high. Back out to the Interstate, down to Colorado Springs, right turn onto US-24 and off to Woodland Park and Pike's Peak.

We got to Pike's Peak shortly after noon and drove up to the top, enjoying the scenery and the sheer drop-offs along the way. It was hard to imagine that they actually hold auto races on this road, without many serious wrecks. The scenery was spectacular and when we got to the top, the sky was so clear it seemed like you should be able to see both the Atlantic and the Pacific Oceans.

We enjoyed a late lunch at the top, while enjoying the scenery. Even though the day had warmed up, there still was some snow that high up. Since there wasn't anything else we wanted to do there, we headed back to Woodland Park, where we planned on staying the night.

"I would like to get my hair cut while we have some time here." Said Becky. "Can we cruise the main drag and see if we can find a salon?"

"Of course. And while you are doing that, I'll find us a place to stay and ask about some place for dinner."

It didn't take long before we found a salon for Becky and as I dropped her off, she said: "Why don't you plan on picking me up in about an hour. I'll look for you out here along the curb."

It didn't take long to find a motel close by and get our bags into the room. The clerk recommended a couple of restaurants that were nearby within walking distance.

After about an hour, I cruised back to the Salon and parked along the curb. Becky wasn't out waiting, so I put the seat back, laid back and closed my eyes. The car door opening woke me, as Becky slid into the car, all smiles and bubbly and gave me a long kiss.

"I know this sounds silly, but it was so nice seeing you sitting here waiting for me." She said. "I got goose bumps all over, I was so happy. Can we go to the motel now? I think I'd like to take a short nap."

"Absolutely," I said. "It isn't far and we have a couple of restaurants to choose from for dinner. I could even use a little nap myself."

As soon as we walked into our room, Becky threw her purse on the table, pushed me against the wall, kissed me long and hard, and said: "I am so hot. I just about creamed my jeans when I saw you waiting for me. I was so happy. It's just like we're a married couple. I can't help myself, I need you now."

Now I have to tell you, she took me by total surprise. I tried to respond, I really did, but try as I might, and try as much as she did, my magic wand stayed limp. No amount of coaxing, even with Becky using her mouth on it, could get it to attention. And I really wanted to make love to her, I just couldn't.

Well, needless to say, our nap was a quiet one with her on one side of the bed and me on the other. And I didn't get much sleep. Dinner was quiet and cool, too. I know she was disappointed, but she wouldn't let me touch her to try to sooth her. We watched a little TV, silently, lying on the bed, where she wouldn't let me hold her or cuddle. I was frozen out.

CHAPTER 26
Wednesday

After an early, quiet breakfast, we got on the road to Aspen, following US-24 most of the way. From Woodland Park across US-24 to Buena Vista is about 70 miles, and half of it is almost like a desert. Because of the time of year there wasn't much traffic, so we had the road pretty much to ourselves.

After we had been on the road for a little while, Becky slid over in the seat and said: "I'm sorry for the way I've been treating you. I know that it isn't as easy for you to get it up as it is for me to get hot. And I know that those things aren't always going to happen together, like yesterday. It's just that I was so excited about you being there and I wanted to celebrate. I really wanted to feel you inside of me. Can you forgive me?"

"Sweetheart," I said. "There's nothing to forgive, other than me for not being able to respond to you. I'm sorry for that, but I don't know why it happened. I do love you, and I wanted to make you happy last night, but something just didn't work. Let's just move on and enjoy the rest of the trip."

"Well, we have a couple of hours until we get to Aspen. Let me see if I can make us both feel better during the ride." She said, as her right hand unbuckled my belt and quickly unzipped me. With my pants laid wide open she massaged my organ until she found some life in it, then she pulled it out of my underpants, laid down on the seat, with her head in my lap, and proceeded to begin licking and sucking my cock to life.

Now I was a willing participant in this adventure, and since the road was a straight line with almost no traffic, I wasn't too concerned about wrecking the car. But to make a long story short (no pun intended), Becky worked on my cock for over a half hour without getting me to cum. After we had crossed the 'desert' area, I knew we were coming up to a major intersection and I was worried that we would be getting more traffic. I found a spot where I could pull off the road, put the seat back a bit and give more attention to Becky. Being able to get one of my hands on one of her tits seemed to help as well.

Shortly after, I cried out: "*Oh! Oh! Yes! We're making progress. I can feel my cock getting harder. I think my cum is on its way. Get ready for a load.*"

Finally, not a gusher, but the result Becky was looking for, I gave her everything I could, stretching out my legs to help push out more of my cum. She had proven that she could get me up and out, and that made her happy, and of course it made me happy too.

After we both got put back together and had hugged and kissed, I put the car seat back where I needed it, to drive, and we went on our way.

Near Buena Vista, US-24 makes a right turn to head north and a few miles later Rte. 82 cuts off to the left and goes over the mountains to Aspen, which is the route we had expected to take.

When we got to the turn for Aspen, we were stopped by a big sign that said:

'Road Closed! Mountain pass full of snow. Take detour.'

This just made the trip a bit longer because we had to continue up US-24, over to Glenwood Springs and then down to Aspen from there. Still, it was a very scenic route without all the snow.

On the way into Aspen, we passed a new area called Snowmass, which I had heard was going to be the next big ski area. Looking up that way, you could see a lot of new construction going on.

CHAPTER 27
Aspen

Pulling into Aspen, it was easy to see why it was so popular. It had the look of an Alpine mountain village. It was an absolutely spectacular setting and the village was so quaint you felt like you had stepped back in time in Switzerland. After parking the car, we strolled the main street until we found an inviting restaurant for lunch.

After lunch we drove to a rustic looking lodge on the edge of town, and arm in arm we strolled inside to inquire about a room. It happened that the owner was at the desk and seeing us, said: "Good afternoon. You look like two love birds on a honeymoon. Can I offer you our honeymoon suite with a King-size bed and a wood burning fireplace? Since its off-season here, I'll let you have it for our regular room rate. I'm sure you'll appreciate it. The view of the mountains from the picture window is spectacular as well."

"We'll take it." We said in unison.

"It sounds perfect," I said.

"Unfortunately, we'll only be staying the one night. Tomorrow we want to drive up to the west entrance of Rocky Mountain National Park."

"That's fine." Said the owner. "We just want you to enjoy your stay with us, so that you'll come back and visit us again. If it's convenient, I'll come to your room around 5 pm and get the fireplace started.

We still have a small kitchen staff on hand, and they can prepare almost any meal you want. If you call down and put your order in ahead of time, I think you will enjoy that too."

"We really appreciate your great hospitality." I said. "After we freshen up, we're going to take a walk around the village and do a bit of sight-seeing.: We should be back here shortly after 5."

That the room was amazing, is an understatement. The setting with the King-size bed, the fireplace, and the luxuriant carpet was a dream room. We both washed up, changed clothes and talked about dinner. Before we left for our walk, I called the restaurant and placed our order for an appetizer of raw oysters, and a dinner of shrimp fettuccini and asparagus tips.

Strolling through Aspen was like going back in time. Old well-kept buildings lined the streets with shops of every description. Surrounded by the sheer rise of mountains all around, with snow-capped peaks. Most of the shops, of course, catered to the ski crowd, but we weren't looking for things to buy, just trying to inhale some of the atmosphere to take back with us. It looked like Aspen could easily live up to its reputation as the perfect winter play-ground.

As 5 O'clock came and passed, the old-time street lights and a few shop lights began to come on. The sun had disappeared sliding over the mountains, like turning off a switch. Looking at the scene as we headed back towards our hotel, you felt like you were walking through a Norman Rockwell painting.

We stopped for a moment to take it in and appreciate the beauty. I turned to Becky, took her in my arms and kissed her long and hard.

"I love you Becky and I'm so happy to be here with you. It's like a dream and we are the only ones in it."

With that she put her head on my shoulder and began to cry.

"These are tears of happiness." She said. "I couldn't imagine being here with anyone but you. I love you with all my heart."

Finally, we turned back towards the hotel and our cozy honeymoon suite. Since we had dinner reservations at 6:30 we didn't want to be late, so we restrained ourselves when we reached our room. We had just enough time to wash up, comb our hair, and sit in front of the fire for a few minutes.

As it turned out, we were the only diners in the restaurant, at this hour, so we had the full service of the chef, who turned out to be our waiter, too. The oysters were properly chilled with a side of horseradish-seasoned seafood cocktail sauce.

"I hope these oysters live up to their reputation as an aphrodisiac." I said to Becky. "I'm beginning to think I may need some help."

"Don't you worry, sweetie." She replied. "I'm going to be the only aphrodisiac you need. Trust me on that."

I guess the owner had passed on to the chef that we might be on our honeymoon, because we had a nicely secluded table, the lights and décor were set to 'romantic' and once our dinner was out, along with a nice bottle of Chardonnay, the chef left us alone.

The dinner was perfect, the setting was perfect and since we were seated side-by-side on a bench seat, we couldn't keep our hands to ourselves. While eating with my right hand, my left hand stayed busy in Becky's lap, first lightly massaging her thighs and crotch, then, since she had slacks on, I slowly unzipped them, slid my hand inside, down into her panties and started massaging her clit directly with a couple of fingers, making her quiver while she was trying to eat.

Not to be left out of the fun, Becky slipped her free hand to the front of my pants, where she found an already hard tool waiting to be unleashed.

"Oh, my!" she exclaimed. "I guess the oysters have been beneficial. I hope you can stay awake long enough tonight to make use of this."

"Honey," I said, "the way I feel right now, we may not get much sleep tonight."

We finished dinner quickly, declining dessert, but taking the wine bottle with us to finish in our room.

"Wait here," Becky said, as we entered our room. "I'll call when I'm ready for you."

Somewhat curious about that, I went and stirred the fire and threw a couple more logs on it. Then I began to undress and get ready for an early shower and a romantic evening.

"Come on in." Becky called from the bathroom.

As I cautiously entered, I saw that she was lying back in the Jacuzzi tub with lots of hot water and suds around her and the bottle of wine along-side on the floor.

"*Wow.*" Was all I could say. She looked so sexy and the tub was so inviting. It took me about 10 seconds to shed the rest of my clothes and climb into the opposite end of the tub.

"Hand me that bottle of wine." I said. "Let's commemorate this day."

With that, we both swigged the rest of the wine while relaxing and luxuriating for our first time together in a hot tub.

I was leaning back with my eyes closed, enjoying the sensation, when I felt Becky's toes begin to massage my crotch, up and down on my pecker, which soon responded, rising like a phoenix from the ashes. Not to be outdone, I let my toes begin to play in her crotch, with my big toe soon finding a home in her pussy, being careful not to scratch her with my toenail.

After a few minutes of this fore-play, I eased my body forward and slid up in the tub, dropping my head under water for a moment to nibble at her clit. Then, sliding all the way up on top of her, I eased my hard cock into her hot pussy and began a slow rocking motion with my ass, trying to make sure we kept our heads above water.

"*Oh, god, that feels so good.*" She said. "Not too fast, I want this to last for a while. You feel so good inside of me, I don't want it to end."

So I tried. I slowed down my motion, even trying to lie quietly for a bit, but the sensation in my groin was just too much and despite my best efforts, I felt myself beginning to come.

"I can't help myself." I said. "You are just too erotic for me. I'm coming now, ready or not." And with that I banged her hard a few more times before shooting my load and relaxing on top of her.

"*Good baby*." She said, kissing me. "That's what I wanted. This one was for you. I know that you have been doing all the work, driving and planning. This was my reward to you for that. I hope you enjoyed it as much as I did."

"*Oh, That was so fantastic. I'm almost speechless.*" I said. "But, rest assured you're not getting off that easy. The combination of the oysters and your sexy body is going to keep us busy most of the night. There will be time for sleeping when we get home."

"*Bring it on, big boy, bring it on.*" She replied, as we climbed out of the tub, toweling each other off, donning the fluffy white hotel robes, and padding in to lay in front of the fire.

Well, it was so warm there and we were both so relaxed, we fell asleep for a while. When I sensed the room growing darker, I got up and put a couple more logs on the fire, which immediately lit the room. The noise awakened Becky and she stretched sexily with her robe parting around her thighs.

As she stood up, she said, "Now you just lay back down here and get comfortable. I've got another little surprise for you. Don't go away."

With that she disappeared into the bathroom with her purse, leaving me to wonder what she was going to do next.

Within a few minutes, Becky was back out, coming over and laying down next to me in front of the fire.

"I brought you a little bit of dessert from the restaurant." She said. "But you have to search for it. Your only clue is that you don't have to leave the room to find it."

Well! That certainly sounded intriguing and inviting. Being a trained observer, I noted that she hadn't brought anything but herself out of the bathroom, so it must be on her body someplace. I guess I would just have to search her.

"I have deduced, with my superior powers of observation, that this 'dessert' must be somewhere on your body. So I'm going to have to search you." I said with a smirk.

"I'm all yours. Do your best and I'm sure you'll get rewarded for your efforts." Said Becky.

So, wanting to prolong the 'search', I began by kissing each ear, not finding anything unusual. Then I moved down to her neck, kissing and nibbling away. As I move on down her body, I undid the belt on her robe and began to fold that back so I could get at her tits and her erect nipples. Tasting each one of these in turn, and then repeating that 'search' again; still nothing.

Spreading her robe more, I moved down to her belly button, gently probing that with my tongue. Still nothing. By now, I had more of a sneaking suspicion, both because of what was left and because my nose was beginning to get a hint of berries.

Not wanting to rush the process, though, I slid all the way down to her feet and nibbled each of her toes.

"Nothing yet." I declared, with a smile, "But I think I'm getting warmer." And by that I meant not only to the 'dessert' but that my joy stick was now standing straight up and was hard again. A fact that I am sure Becky had observed.

Spreading the rest of her robe open, I moved up Becky's legs to her thighs where my tongue soon found the 'dessert'. She had spread raspberry jam around her pussy and mixed it in with her fine hairs. My 'dessert' was to eat all of it and 'clean the plate', which I proceeded to do. While I was busy 'eating', I made sure that my tongue went to work on her clit and soon had her squirming, humping my face, and moaning.

Soon she took my head in her hands and pulled me up so that my rod was at her door.

"That's enough 'dessert' for you," she said. "*Time for my dessert now*. Fuck me as hard as you can, because I'm not going to take long to come. I almost orgasmed while you were eating your dessert."

With that, she rolled me over, sat up on my lap and proceeded to do a dance on my prick.

True to her words, she soon cried. *"Anytime now, you can join me. I'm going to explode. Come on baby. Make momma happy tonight."*

"I'm ready sweet-cheeks. Let's see what you've got. You first then I'll follow. I want to feel your juices flow." I replied.

With that she arched her back and went stiff with her orgasm, slowly rocking like she had one, then two, and finally three spasms. After her second spasm, I pushed up and started pumping my butt until I brought myself to a peak and blew my load. As I began to relax, I felt her third spasm, then she fell on top of me, completely spent.

Silence for several minutes, then she said: *"Oh, sugar, what did you do to me?* I feel like I've been working out all day. I don't think I can even stand."

"I was just having my 'dessert' when I was attacked by a wild woman." I said. "I'm not sure that I can stand, either, but maybe we can crawl over to the bed and climb in."

Which we did, and went right to sleep in our, now, traditional 'spoon' position.

CHAPTER 28
Thursday - On the road again.

I would like to say that I woke up with 'morning wood' again, but I didn't. Limp as a dish rag and even a little sore. Climbing out of bed and wobbling into the bathroom to pee, I decided that I would just shave and shower while I was there.

Coming back into the bedroom, I saw that Becky was still sound asleep. I quietly dressed, left the room, went down to the lobby and out to a nearby coffee shop to pick up bagels and coffee.

Back in the room, I gently shook Becky, saying: "Time to get up sleepy-head. Breakfast is on the table."

To which she replied: "Were we in a whirlwind last night? I feel like I've been ravaged and tossed around. I'm not sure that I can walk this morning."

The coffee helped both of us perk back up, and shortly we checked out, got back in the car and on the road again. Our goal today was to drive to Vail, stopping for lunch there, then after a little sight-seeing, continue on to the west entrance to the Rocky Mountain National Park.

As we reluctantly left Aspen, Becky curled up on the seat with her head in my lap again, but this time she was asleep before we passed Snowmass.

It was an easy drive over to Vail, and I woke Becky just before we pulled into town.

We were a little disappointed after seeing Aspen, because Vail was sort of crammed in between a couple of mountains and didn't have any of the old-world appeal that Aspen had. After cruising around to get a feel for the village, we parked and began to stroll around the cobblestone streets.

It was easy to see that, unlike Aspen, Vail had been built from the ground up for skiers. And it probably deserved its reputation as one of the premier ski areas in the world. The mountains were just as spectacular, with some ski slopes still covered with snow. It just wasn't our 'cup of tea'

Eventually we found a quaint little coffee shop with a decent menu and had a quick lunch. Then it was back to the car and on down the road. According to the map, it should be about a three hour drive to Grand Lake, which is the western entrance to Rocky Mountain National Park. Grand Lake also is near where the mighty Colorado River starts its journey to the sea.

While I was enjoying the scenery and remarking about the great weather we had during the trip, Becky had begun rubbing the inside of my thigh. It didn't take long before I felt myself responding and I started squirming around on the seat, because my pants were getting tight.

"Are you having a problem?" queried Becky. "Let's see if I can make you more comfortable." With that she pulled down my zipper, unbuckled my belt and probed around with her hand until she had a good grip on my prick.

"Here's your problem." She snickered. "You've gone and gotten yourself a hard-on, haven't you?"

"Well, you've had something to do with that. Now that you have ahold of it, what do you intend to do to make me more comfortable?"

"Hmm, let me ponder that for a second." She snickered, again. "I think I know just the remedy. Just don't lose control of the car. OK?"

With that she slid down on the seat, again, put her head over my lap and proceeded to deep-throat me.

"*Oh, baby.*" I said, "You certainly do have the technique for making me comfortable. It's a good thing the road is straight with no traffic, though."

After our exertions of the night before, I knew this was going to be another prolonged blow-job, so I slowed the car a bit and tried to get more into the mood.

After about twenty minutes of ministrations, Becky came up for air, saying:

"How about putting your mind to it and try to help me out here?" Then she went back at it.

It wasn't long before we closed in on the back of a Greyhound bus, chugging up the road. Without thinking too much about it, I sped up and passed him quickly, then settled back down to a reasonable speed.

Soon I felt myself getting ready to unload and I cried out: "*OK, you win. Here I come baby. Take it all down. OH! yes! yes! take it deep. That's the way. OH! I think you got everything that time. That was great.*"

After I had gone limp, Becky dropped me from her mouth and sat up, stuffing me back into my underpants and pulling up my zipper.

It was then that I looked in the rearview mirror and saw a state police cruiser closing in fast behind us. Becky was upright and I was half-presentable so I didn't think much about it. I thought he was probably heading on up the road.

"Stay sitting up," I said, "We have a trooper coming up behind us."

"OK!" she replied, "I'm presentable."

Well, the trooper pulled up pretty close behind us and then just stayed there for about 10 minutes, and I was beginning to get a little nervous.

"Maybe the bus drive saw more than I thought he could, when I pulled around him." I said. "He could have put in a call about what he saw."

But then, it wasn't long that the trooper pulled over to the side, did a U-turn and headed back south.

"I would have to think that the bus driver did put in a call to them. He probably was jealous" Said Becky. "It's a good thing you finally delivered, before the cops arrived. If my head had still been down, he probably would have pulled us over.

CHAPTER 29
Grand Lake

Pulling into Grand Lake, I was too spent to try driving on into the Park, so we stopped at the first decent looking motel and checked in.

I promptly stretched out on the bed, closed my eyes and slept for a couple of hours.

"Wake up sleepy-head." Becky said as she shook me lightly. "Its time to eat. I'm hungry after all the 'work' I did today."

"My love," I replied, "you can 'work' on me anytime you want. I just needed a little shut-eye to refresh me. Have you looked for a place to eat?"

"Yes, I have," Becky responded, "in fact there is a cute little diner just across the street. I'd like to try that. Then maybe we can take a walk along the lake. The mountains around the lake are amazing."

"Just let me wash my face, and I'll be ready to go." I said.

"This 'cute little diner' has an interesting menu." I commented after we were seated. "I see that they have oysters on the half shell. Oysters must be a favorite with the skiers around here. I think that I can use another half dozen of them myself."

"Maybe you should have a dozen." snickered Becky. "I'm not done with you yet, you know."

"Bring it on sweetie, bring it on. I'll do my best to keep up with you. I don't want you to lose interest in me and go off looking for a 'hunk' skier."

"My love," she replied, "don't lose any sleep over that thought. You are the only one that I want, and I'll try not to wear you out, *after this trip is over*. Here and now is a different matter though. So go for those oysters. You're going to need them."

And I did. I ordered and downed a dozen of them.

Later, walking off some of the calories from our dinner, we talked about what was left of our trip.

"Friday is our last full day of sight-seeing." I said. "How would you like to drive up into the Park and do some light, easy hiking and see if we can see some moose, that I understand are around this area."

"Sounds good to me." Replied Becky. "I'm going to take along a sweater and a jacket, though. It is a bit cooler up here than some of the other places we've been."

"Well, there's no need to be in a hurry in the morning either. We need to let the dew get off the ground before we head out, so we don't get wet feet. We can sleep in if we want to, then have a late breakfast." I said.

"The sun is going down behind the mountains now, so we should head back to our room, and see if we can find something to do." She said with a grin.

"Oh, I brought along a book to read if things got too dull." I snidely remarked. "And you have your knitting."

"Maybe, *just maybe*, I'll let you read tonight. If you promise to have another nice wake-up surprise for me in the morning.

"I'll do my best." I said. "That's all I can promise. Sometimes I don't have any control over how I wake up. Although, I must say, it has been happening a lot more often sleeping with you in my arms."

CHAPTER 30
Friday

Even though there was a lot of hugging and kissing when we went to bed, and I was getting all 'hot and bothered', Becky finally turned over, backed up into my arms and soon was asleep.

I have to admit that I slept like the proverbial 'log', but when morning dawned, there it was, my 'morning wood'. I was so hard and my erection was pressing into Becky's back, so I was surprised she wasn't awake. Sliding one hand up to her breasts, I began playing with her nipples, feeling them come hard and erect. Then I slid my hand down to her soft, blond pussy and gently fingered her lips, inserting a couple of fingers gently inside to arouse her clit.

"OH! Is it morning already?" she moaned. "What are you doing to me so early. I thought we were going to sleep in."

"OK." I said quickly, removing my hand form her crotch. "Go back to sleep."

"*Don't you dare*." She almost shouted, as she put my hand back. "You woke me up, now you have to finish what you started."

So, lifting her leg, I slid my cock into her pussy, while my fingers massaged her clit. Within a few minutes, I could feel her stiffen and stretch as an orgasm rolled through her. Sometimes she was so easy.

Turning her over to face me, I rolled onto my back and in the same motion, pulled her up onto me, so she was sitting on my lap facing me, with my erection standing up in front of her.

"Well, well." she said. "I see those oysters must have been worth the price. You seem to still have a hard-on for me."

"It's all yours, sweetheart. Do with me what you will. Do you think you can handle all of that this morning?"

"Just stay focused." She said as she gripped my cock, and began a slow hand-job. "I'm going to drain you dry this morning."

"How does this feel?" she asked, as she raised up slightly and let herself down, engulfing me. "I'm going to give you the lap-dance of your lifetime. Just lie still and keep that meat at attention."

With that, she sat up straight, closed her eyes, cupped her hands behind her hair, gathering it up on her head, and seemed to go into a trance for a few moments. Slowly and quietly she began humming what sounded like some of the music from Scheherazade. Then she started 'dancing' on my lap keeping time to her humming. Sometimes slow and writhing, then picking up the pace like she was following the conductor, suddenly getting frenetic and wild, all with her eyes closed.

After about 5 minutes of this 'dance', I could feel myself getting absorbed by her performance, and I could feel the juices in my groin starting to rise.

"*Oh, baby,*" I cried. "*I'm coming. Don't stop, don't stop, come with me, hurry, come with me now.*" And with that I exploded and flooded her to the point where I could feel juices running out of her and down my legs.

"Oh, lover," she cried. "You got me again too. *You big devil, you.*" Then collapsing on me and rolling over onto her back, she said: "We're going to have to change the sheets for sure."

After a late breakfast, we drove up into the Park, with bag lunches from the diner. Inquiring from the gate-keeper about the best trails to see moose, he recommended taking the Coyote Trail about 6 miles inside the Park. It was an easy trail with little climbing and it was a common route. As with any of the trails, it was very scenic with plenty of places to stop and rest or to eat lunch. He also reminded us that the Park was a 'trash in, trash out' park, which helped maintain the pristine nature of the park and made it more enjoyable for other visitors.

It was an even more enjoyable hike than we had expected. We took our time, tried to stay quiet so as not to spook any animals and followed the trail. Shortly after starting out, we found ourselves walking along the bank of the Colorado River. We were in a great meadow with mountains around, which we saw from the map were called the Never Summer Mountains.

I had brought along my fly rod, just to try some 'catch and release' in the Colorado River. Becky had brought her knitting, which so far hadn't progressed a lot. So we found a spot with a picnic table near the river and settled down there.

I did manage to pull a few trout out of the river over the course of the early afternoon. Stopping for a time to eat lunch and make encouraging comments about Becky's sweater project which now was beginning to take shape.

As we sat at the table, Becky lightly touched my arm and motioned up the river, where three moose had come out of the woods and were at the river. We watched them as they waded through river and grazed their way across the meadow until they disappeared into the trees. What magnificent animals! I had never seen one before and now three at once.

Just as I was getting up to go back and try my luck at fishing again, I spotted a couple of red fox running across another part of the meadow. This was the reason we wanted to come up here. It was quiet and peaceful, and warm enough to walk around; gorgeous scenery and the 'frosting' was being able to see some rare animals in their natural habitat. What a great last day to our trip.

When the sun started over the western mountains, it began to cool down, so we headed back to the car and drove back to Grand Lake.

Dinner at the diner was similar to the night before. I started off with a dozen oysters, then I decided to have a nice piece of western beef in the form of a strip steak. Becky went for the shrimp and scallop special, so we got to sample each other's meal, like lovers do.

We walked along the lake, arm in arm again, enjoying the serenity and the late evening glow of the sky. Snuggled together on a bench along-side the lake, we watched the stars come out and then watched a huge golden moon slowly creep up over the eastern mountain range. What a scene for our last night out here.

"We need to talk about life back home, before we leave." I said. "My desire is that we move in together. Not in our current homes, but in a new one just for us. I'm not sure what the timing should be, though. How do you feel about that?"

"I would like that," replied Becky, "I don't see any reason to put it off, though. It will take some time to find a place and complete the purchase. I don't have to be out of my apartment for six months, but I would rather not stay in it. Would it be a problem for you if I sort of moved in with you now?"

"That wouldn't be a problem with me. I would love having you there every morning when I wake up. This late in the school year, you probably can't sublet your apartment, but you could leave any larger items there until we find our new home. I still have to get rid of all of Jackie's stuff, but I think I'll just box it all up and take it to Goodwill. If we can find a furnished house to buy, I'll have a household sale and sell all my current furniture. There isn't anything that I am attached to. If we can't find a furnished one, we'll just buy new furniture."

"Sounds like a plan to me." Said Becky, "I'm getting chilled though, I'd like to go back to our room so we can make love one more time before we leave."

"*That* sounds like a plan that I like." I quickly said, as I stood and pulled her up.

And make love we did, slow and with tenderness, in the light of a couple of flickering candles. No hurry, each one trying to please the other. When we climaxed together we just lay in each other's arms, kissing and hugging until we fell asleep.

CHAPTER 31
Saturday

We were awakened by the sun starting to shine in through our window. Both surprised that we had slept so long. Becky turned over to face me, and realized that I had an enormous erection, again, that was poking her in the stomach.

"Do you wake up this way every morning.?" She quipped. "Or are you just happy to see me?"

"Well, this isn't unusual, but it certainly has been happening more with you around, then I ever remember before." I replied,

"Well, let me see if I can alleviate your discomfort." She quipped again, as she slid down in the bed and took me in her mouth.

As much as she tried, for about 10 minutes, she couldn't get me to blow, so she stopped, took me in hand and tried that for a while. Another 10 minutes or so and I was still holding out and still rock solid. Those oysters must have been potent.

It was beginning to warm up in the cabin, partly because of the sun, but mostly because both of us were beginning to perspire from Becky's efforts.

"I'm not going to leave you in this condition." She said. "You're going to be mine, even if it takes all day." And with that she eased up on my lap and dropped down onto my cock with a moan of pleasure. "Let's have a little cooperation now," she said, "We don't have all day, you know, we do have to get down to Denver tonight. "

I can't begin to tell how much I tried to cooperate and shoot my load, but after about a half hour of trying and an orgasm, Becky collapsed against my chest, which by now was soaked with sweat. Then I realized that Becky was soaked and the sheets around us were soaked as well.

Since Becky had been doing most of the 'work', I gently rolled her over while staying inside her.

"Let's see what I can do." I said. "Help out where you can." With that I tried to position myself to get the most 'friction' from our coupling, and began to bang her as hard as I could.

As I was doing this, I felt both of her hands gripping my ass, pulling me into her even more. Then one of her hands slid over to my a-hole and I felt a finger snaking up inside of me. Soon she found the spot she was looking for and began to massage me from the inside.

Well, this was something new to me and it had a remarkable effect. No sooner had she begun working me with her finger, than I felt myself began to gather for an explosion. And when I came, it was a mind blowing, earth shattering event. I felt Becky shudder as my load hit inside of her, then I felt a responding orgasm from her that seemed to go on for minutes. Finally, we both fell exhausted to the soggy bed. Too tired to move, too tired to talk.

Soon, though, I wrapped my arms about her and rolled over with her to a drier side of the bed and pulled the sheet up over us. "That was a wonderful 'climax' to our trip." I whispered in her ear.

"It surely was." She mumbled.

We fell asleep that way for about an hour, then I got up and went to get a shower. While I was dressing, Becky showered. Then we hobbled slowly over to the diner for a brunch, before checking out and heading for Denver. It was a fitting culmination to the whole trip.

We made a slow drive down to Denver, still enjoying the grand scenery, which we probably wouldn't see again for a while. After checking into our motel, we ate an early dinner, then went right to bed and to sleep. Both of us were too worn out, from our morning exercise, to even consider making love. We had an 8 am flight heading back East and wanted to get to the airport without having to rush.

WEEK FIVE
Home again

CHAPTER 32
Sunday

The flight back was smooth and uneventful. I think we both slept most of the way, waking just before the plane landed. I took the shuttle to pick up my car while Becky waited for the luggage. We got back to the garage, where Becky had left her car, and it was sitting outside waiting for her.

"Do you want to come to my place and stay tonight?" I asked.

"I think I had better go to my place." She replied. "I need to get some clothes ready for work tomorrow and make sure that I get some sleep. As wonderful as this trip has been, it has been exhausting, especially the last few days."

"OK." I said, giving her a long kiss and hug. "Drive carefully, sleep tight, and I'll see you at the office in the morning. I love you, Becky."

"I love you, Big Boy, even though you have been so rough on me this week." She replied. "We can talk about timing during lunch tomorrow."

CHAPTER 32
Monday

"I'm going to take an extended lunch hour today." I said to Becky, when we met in her office first thing on Monday morning. "I have some personal business that I have to take care of. Then I have to meet with my department manager and make plans for the next phase of my project. So I may not get to see you much here today. Can we get together for dinner at Luigi's tonight?"

"That will work great for me. I have to do the monthly maintenance on the computer, so I'm going to be busy all day, too. It's going to be nice getting back to Luigi's where *we* started."

After a long kiss and hug, I went to my office and sat at my desk organizing the project material for this afternoon. When I had that in my briefcase and ready to go, I slipped out the hallway door and left the building.

My first stop was at Luigi's where I asked Luigi to reserve our usual table and to put a bottle of Moët & Chandon Champagne on ice for us. I expected this to be a night to remember.

My second stop was at a downtown jewelry store, where I picked out a nice diamond engagement ring and put that in my pocket for later.

My next stop was at the realtor's office, where I met with the realtor who had sold me my current house. I told her that I was putting my house up for sale and that I would be looking for a new house, but didn't have any guidelines for her yet, other than a general price range.

Then I stopped at the local thrift store to see if they had pick-up service for a lot of second-hand clothes and some other odds and ends. After they agreed to that, I told them that everything would be boxed up by the following Monday.

My last stop was at my department manager's office, where we spent the afternoon reviewing the project status, the schedule for the next three months and my budget needs. George was pleased with my progress and my schedule and that made me feel good.

By the time I had covered all of these tasks, it was after 5 pm, so I headed over to Luigi's to get a shot of scotch to try to calm me down for this evening's dinner.

CHAPTER 33
Engagement Dinner

I nursed my drink, at the bar, until I saw Becky enter. Then I ordered a Chivas on the rocks for her, too.

Luigi led her to our table, which he had taken personal care in setting up for the evening.

As Luigi left the table, I walked in and sat down on the bench-seat, next to Becky. After putting her glass of scotch on the table, I gave her a long hug and kiss. "How did your day go?" I asked.

"I didn't even have time to stop for lunch," she replied. "I'm famished. How was your day? Did you get all of your *personal* tasks done?"

"Yes, I did. I even took time to stop by the realtor and put my house up for sale. With everything else, I only got here a few minutes before you."

"Well, thanks for having my drink ready. I can really use that right now."

"You know," she continued. "you look like the cat that just caught a bird. You have this silly look on your face. Are you up to something that I should know about?"

"Me? Up to something? Perish the thought."

"Oh, good," I said. "here's Luigi with our dinner; I took the liberty of pre-ordering for us. I hope surf-and-turf is ok with you. We enjoyed it on the trip, so I thought it would be good tonight."

"Surf-and-turf sounds really good, *that was so thoughtful of you to plan this*. You're not trying to put me in a good mood, so you can take advantage of me tonight, are you?" she said, with a grin.

"Well, that might have crossed my mind." I replied. "But I wouldn't try to *force* you to do anything you didn't want to do."

"OK, just so you know, I don't drop my drawers for every cute guy that comes along and buys me a meal and a drink."

As the waiter was clearing our table after dinner, Luigi walked over with two champagne glasses and the bottle of Champagne in an ice bucket. "*Complements of the House, my friends.*" He said, as he poured our first glass and then turned and walked away.

"Well, well, isn't this a surprise." I remarked as we touched glasses and kissed lightly.

"I wonder what's gotten into Luigi?" Becky said. "He's being especially solicitous tonight. Do you think it's because he missed us?"

"Well, it could be that, or it could be this." I said, as I pulled the box with the ring out of my pocket.

"I know that it is very early in our relationship. And I know that neither of us will be free for a few months, but I wanted to do something to let you know how strongly I feel about you. Not just sexually, which has been great, but personally too. I want you to know that I want to spend the rest of my life with you. Will you be the love of my life and agree to spend the rest of your life with me?"

I said as I opened the box and held the ring out to her.

"*OH, my god! I had no idea*. You've really managed to surprise me." She exclaimed, as the tears started running down her cheeks.

"*Yes! Yes!*" she continued. "I can't imagine life without you now. I will gladly be the love of your life, *forever*."

"I'm in shock, though. I really wasn't expecting this. I'm speechless. You had better find some place to take me to make love to me now, though, or I'll rip your clothes off right here at the table."

Leaving quickly, with a thumbs-up to Luigi, we drove over to the Red Roof Inn, where I had already booked a room for the night.

I was just able to get the door shut and latched when Becky was working at my belt buckle. "Get these clothes off," she said, as she started shedding hers. "*To hell with the shower, tonight*. I can't wait that long for you. I want you to fuck me as long and as hard as

186

you can. And you'd better have it hard right now."

"Not to worry, my love." I said, as I picked her up in my arms and carried her to the bed. "I'm at attention already and I'll gladly fuck you as long and as hard as I can last. And then again in the morning."

With that I placed her at the edge of the bed and immediately impaled her on my cock, pushing her up onto the bed where I proceeded to fuck her as hard as I could.

"*OH! god, more! more! don't stop, Harder, harder.* Give me all you've got big boy. Please don't stop. *OH!, yes!, yes!, that feels so good. OH!, god, I'm coming, I'm coming, NOW!*"

Even though I felt that I could 'blow' in the first couple of minutes, I had managed to hold off until Becky was ready, so we could come together.

"*I'm with you, babe, I'm with you now. Here I come.*" I hollered, and with another mind blowing, earth shattering explosion we came together, both shuddering and shaking until I thought the bed was going to fall down.

"*Ohhhh, my, you sure know how to treat a girl.* That was incredible. How can our love making just keep getting better all the time? You're going to have a lot to live up to after this."

"It takes two to make it work." I said. "I've never had this much feeling and this much 'energy' with anyone else before."

"You are something special, and that's why I want us to be together." I said. "I think that we found, on our trip, that we could spend long periods of time together, without getting bored. I want to take it to the next level. I want you to move in with me, *now*. Before we find *our* house.

"I'm going to buy a new bed this week." I continued. "A bed that will be just ours. Then I want you to come over and help me *break it in*. Bring as many clothes as you want, the closets will be empty and clean. You will still have your apartment if you feel that you need some space once in a while."

"I talked with a realtor this morning. I told her that my house was for sale and that I was looking for a new one. Do you have a preference on what side of town you live, or what style of house you want?"

"I would really like to live just outside of town, with some land." Said Becky. "I think maybe a ranch-style, one floor, in excellent condition. I don't want us to have to be remodeling or fixing things all the time. It could even be a new house."

"OK. I'll give our preferences to the realtor and have them do the preliminary selection. I should be able to bring photos and specs. on some 'possibilities' for the two of us to review and when we see one that appears to fit, we can do a drive-by before we ask for a walk-through."

"That sounds great. This is so exciting." She said. "A new beginning and so much to look forward to. I'm so happy with you. You have to promise me you won't get tired of me."

CHAPTER 34

The new bed arrived within a few days and the old bed was taken away the same day.

That weekend Becky moved some of her clothes and personal items over to my house, and we began the process of everyday living together.

The first night that she moved in we made an elaborate ritual of going to bed.

I went first and showered and then sat in the bedroom trying to read, but the suspense was killing me and I couldn't remember what I had read.

Becky came up, and spent about a half hour in the bathroom, showering and fixing her hair.

While she was in the shower, I lit a couple of aromatic candles in the bedroom. As she came out of the bathroom, dressed in a filmy negligee, I went to her, picked her up in my arms, kissed her and carried her to the bed. Having pulled back the blanket and sheet, I laid her on the bed and then I lay down next to her.

"This is a special night for us." I said, "I want it to be one that we will remember for a long time. I love you, Becky, and I always will."

"I love you to Jerry," she replied. "This has been a whirlwind romance, but I have no doubt in my mind, that I will love you for the rest of my life."

As we kissed and hugged, I began running my hand gently up and down her body, stopping for a while to roll her nipples in my fingers and to gently massage her breasts.

As I felt her body responding to my touch, I moved my hand down to her thighs and began slowly massaging her pussy. As I was doing this, Becky slid her hand down my chest until she found my already hard erection.

After a few light strokes, she slid down and took my in her mouth, lubricating my pole along its entire length. I lay back, just enjoying her ministrations, until I felt that I was getting too close to exploding.

Pulling her back up next to me, I slid down, kissing her nipples, then kissing my way down to her thighs, where I was greeted by her already lubricated pussy lips. Pulling her pussy lips into my mouth I began gently sucking and nibbling, occasionally sliding my tongue deep into her honey pot. Soon she was moaning and writhing around on the bed.

"Stop, stop, please, I want you inside of me now. I need to feel all of you in me. I want us to come together, tonight."

Sliding my body up along hers I felt my cock at her pussy lips and gently slid it in as far as it would go.

"*OH, that feels so good*." She said. "Now fuck me, as hard as you can, I want to feel your manhood tonight."

Banging her as hard and as fast as I could, it only took a few minutes until we both exploded in another mind blowing, earth shattering climax. We had not been together for a few days, and I had a lot of stored-up cum to give her.

When we were finished, exhausted and trying to get our breathing under control, we realized that we were lying in a huge wet spot, so we moved to the other side of the bed, pulled the sheet over us and fell asleep in each other's arms.

CHAPTER 35
A New Home

After a few weeks of looking at several houses, we found a relatively new house, which the owners had to sell because of a job transfer. The house was in almost mint condition and was sitting on several acres of land just two miles out of town.

We purchased the house, jointly, then had a cleaning service come in and give it a thorough cleaning. While that was going on, we purchased new furniture, which ensured that it was, in fact, *our house*.

When all was ready, we drove out to the house and walked up to the front door. Pulling the key from my pocket, I unlocked the door and swung it open.

"Ms. Blake. If you will allow me the pleasure." I said, as I picked her up in my arms, and carried her over the threshold. As I shut the door with my foot, we kissed, long and hard.

Still kissing, I stood her in the middle of the room. Coming up for air, I said: "Welcome to our new home, to our growing love, and to our future together."

"Well, our realtor left us a house-warming gift." Becky said, "I think this is the appropriate time to open it."

Opening the refrigerator, we found the bottle of Champagne, popped the cork, and toasted our new life together.

The End